P9-BIH-016

Outside Eden

By the Same Author

POEMS IN ONE VOLUME

A FACE IN CANDLELIGHT
AND OTHER POEMS

COLLECTED PARODIES

TRICKS OF THE TRADE

THE GRUB STREET NIGHTS ENTERTAINMENTS
(Short Stories)

Outside Eden

By J. C. Squire

Alfred A. Knopf
New York   1933

Printed in Great Britain
at The Windmill Press, Surrey

TO
CECILY SEVERNE

CONTENTS

NOTE

ONE of these stories appeared in *The Fothergill Omnibus* (Eyre & Spottiswoode), and one in *If* (Longmans). I thank these publishers and the editors of *Harpers*, *The Strand*, and *The Windsor* for originally printing some of these stories. The editor of the *London Mercury* had no option.

"THIS BLOODY TURF"

"THIS BLOODY TURF"

WHEN a man has made a large pile he will, if he is sensible, try to become respectable. One man will buy acres he cannot farm, hunters he cannot ride, and pheasants he cannot shoot. Another will collect pictures which, according to the advice of chance friends or dealers, or the whim of his wife, may be the work either of the oldest masters or the newest impostors. Another will devote himself to some special sphere of patriotic endeavour—cancer, consumption, or the Olympic Games. And a man who happens to have made a fortune in the theatre, will certainly, in order to vindicate himself, begin to take an interest in the Art of the Drama. This may be manifested in one of three kinds of production: that of ancient plays (including those of Shakespeare), that of plays by sombre or bewildering modern foreigners, or that of new poetic tragedies, preferably blank verse by neglected British geniuses.

Mr. Stanley Gudgeon, arriving at a time when the first two forms of enterprise had been lately rather overdone, and no new British play in blank verse had been put on for fully five years, naturally decided to do what, by lapse of time, had once more become the really original and striking thing. He therefore announced to his friends in the Press, and they to a listening world, that he was determined to bring poets back into the theatre, and that he proposed to consider for six months any poetic plays that might be submitted to him, and at the end of the period, put on the best of them at one of his five theatres, with a fine cast and all the resources of the modern producer's art. Once more, thought thousands of idealists, as they rustled the pages of their morning papers, a new epoch had opened in the history of the British Stage. The new Elizabethan age was once more about to arrive. A theatre given over to trivial buffoonery, shallow smartness, cynical immorality and clumsy thrills, was once more to be purged and made the fit arena for all that is nobly passionate in the human soul, and all that is most melodious in human language.

Mr. Stanley Gudgeon had spoken; and, after all, if you cannot believe a man who has made a half a million in two years, whom can you believe?

The public was given to understand—"reminded" was the polite word most commonly used—that it was this renovation of the theatre which had always been Mr. Gudgeon's aim. Paragraphists, sketching his "meteoric" career, began to make it plain. They made the whole career so plain and deliberate, indeed, that it acquired, in retrospect, a kind of inevitability, like that of a figure in epic, fixed in ultimate intention and protected by the gods.

The actual facts of the career were these. Stanley Gudgeon was the son of a respectable Nonconformist grocer in North—or perhaps it was South—Shields, and after spending some time at the local Grammar School without distinguishing himself, proceeded to the local University College. There, nominally, he studied in the School of English Literature, developing, as time went on, a taste for Art, Aubrey Beardsley and the Modern Theatre, though no great mastery over the language of Chaucer, or the doctrines of *Areopagitica*, which were the sort of things he was expected to work up for examinations. That he was set apart mysteriously from his fellows was already evident to him: he made it palpable to them by growing his hair longer and longer, and mooning about with his shoulders hunched and a smouldering fire in his dark eyes. He was tall, and, at this time, thin, and although his nose was short and parakeetish and his other features not very strongly marked, the more imaginative of the young women students already detected in him, not without awe, a resemblance to the late Sir Henry Irving which was precisely what he hoped to achieve. What more natural than that, when (chiefly owing to the enthusiasm of these young women) a University Dramatic Society was started, Mr. Stanley Gudgeon should become first secretary, then chairman of the selection

B

committee; then producer, principal actor, general manager, and, in fact, general autocrat? The natural thing naturally occurred. Stanley opened his first season with a drama by Henry Arthur Jones. While this was still in rehearsal, the whole cast being wild about its beauties, he realised that this was not the sort of thing for a pioneer; and in his later productions he drove steadily onward and upward, through Mr. A. A. Milne and Sir James Barrie to Mr. Galsworthy, Mr. Shaw and Euripides (via Professor Murray), and his last play of all showed that he had really reached the penetralia of the Dramatic Renaissance. He first tried to induce the Committee to let him put on Ibsen's *Ghosts*: they understood it, were afraid of the Governors and the parents, and refused. But he then procured copies of a German Expressionist play which the Committee understood no more than he did. The play had been greatly praised by certain London writers, with whose panegyrics he had armed himself; nobody liked to admit inability to perceive the splendours underlying the surface gibberish of the thing, and, for three solid hours all the rank and fashion of North (unless it was South) Shields sat, as in a church, staring at a number of cubical designs and listening to a disjointed variety of hammerings, rattling and cryptic interjections. This was the turning-point. Stanley, the parental purse dry, hopes of a degree abandoned, even forgotten, nothing in view except the vague prospect of a fortnight's stay in London with a college friend, who had got to know a man on a theatrical newspaper, suddenly established a liaison with Mr. Richard Grunt, Jnr., of Grunts, the largest ironmasters in North, or as it may be South, Shields.

Mr. Edward Grunt, a plump, pink, prosperous, round-headed, fair-moustached man of forty, had married a woman who was the undisputed queen of Shieldian intellectual society. The match was a very suitable one, as he himself had distinctly intellectual leanings: he had discovered for himself several of the novels of Mr. Wells, and had been heard to remark when quite young and a bachelor, "That chap Bernard Shaw's a very clever fellow." He had been, like many of his fellows among the aristocracy of the town, to a Midland public school; but had left early to go into the business, the sole evidences of his education being a mitigated accent, a polished heartiness of manner, and a notable Old Boy's tie. Poorer friends often told each other with awe that he was reputed to have a standing order with the school haberdasher for a new tie every month. The atmosphere of the play-house he had always liked. He was a regular stall-buyer at the local theatre, and invariably went to the play when visiting London.

At the time of his marriage he had already graduated out of the school of musical comedy into that of middle-brow drama: his wife broadened his outlook still farther. She, the daughter of the principal local doctor, took seriously the view that the age should and would be reformed by its dramatists, and it was a grievance to her that enforced residence in the cramping provinces prevented her from having an adequate finger in the pie. As it was, she had got herself and her husband elected members of the Sunday Mummers, that most chic and unsuccessful of London play-producing societies; she contrived at least twice a year to dragoon the local Literary and Philosophical Society to pay the fee of some young man from London with a message concerning Strindberg, Wedekind and other Light-Bringers; and no guest ever slept at her house without finding on his bedroom table, with the daffodils, roses, or chrysanthemums (according to season) odd volumes of Hauptmann, Sudermann, Hudermann, Brudermann and Still von Rudermann.

*   *   *   *

There came a night, Mr. Grunt, ruddy, well-tailored, well-dined, and Mrs. Grunt, undoubtedly better dressed than anybody else in either of the Shieldses, sat in the front row at Stanley Gudgeon's last performance as Lord High Panjandrum of the University Dramatic Society. The play, translated from the Lithuanian, was undoubtedly difficult, but undoubtedly pregnant with significance. The young men, driven by Stanley, went through their parts vigorously if not very comprehendingly; the young women, resolved to rise to the heights of Stanley's vast understanding, raved and tremoloed superbly, for all the world as though their parts meant, not merely something, but everything, to them. Calm, in the midst of them all, was Stanley: selector, manager, producer, principal actor, sailing serenely through the leading part (that of a railway clerk named Czczcz, who was challenging the Almighty on behalf of all mankind) like a Triton among the minnows. Mrs. Grunt loved her husband, or at any rate liked him enough not to love anybody else, at any rate too much. But love, like, admire, respect him as she might; grateful though she might be for his reliability, his sense, his sympathy and his income; she could, nevertheless, not help feeling—and indefinable electric thrills went through her whenever he was on the stage and challenging the Universe in that deep, rich, rolling voice of his—that Stanley Gudgeon was different from anybody else whom she had ever encountered. There was no question of love; their souls met, without bodily contact, without speech even, in an Upper Air, inhabited only by the few who truly Perceive, Feel and Understand. She knew it in every quaver of his speech, in every quick glance of his eye: this (for she herself was aware of rare genius) was an affinity: she could do nothing else for him (as she was married to Grunt and the Ironworks) but she could at least serve

him, and make possible the full flowering of his
genius. That that might result in some exquisite
intimate relation between them (something tenuous
and poetic and renunciatory, over the head of the
worthy podgy Grunt, but never, never, even tinged
with disloyalty to him) may have fluttered across her
mind like a butterfly across a garden, but she knew
that that wasn't really influencing her at all. No:
Gudgeon with his genius, she with only her humble
desire to serve and her unique power of judging
player and play: they were fellow-servants of Art, and
Art was all.

That night, slipping off her cloth-of-silver in her
bedroom, she called to her husband, who was dis-
banding his white tie in the adjoining dressing-room.

"Ted," she cried, "come here."

"Right you are, darling," he replied, appearing at
the door, "what is it?"

"D'you mind, darling," she went on, "sleeping in
your own room to-night?"

"Why, of course not," replied he; "I'm not at all
sleepy and I'll get on with Boswell."

"Oh, your wretched old Boswell," she proceeded
impatiently; and then, with a touch of coquetry, "but I
suppose he seems different to you men. But look here,
darling."

"Yes, darling."

"You *did* enjoy to-night, didn't you?"

"Why, of course I did: I enjoy absolutely anything if you are there."

"Ted, I didn't mean that. I mean, you *did* think that both the play and Mr. Gudgeon were marvellous, *didn't* you?"

"Oh, my dear, of course I did. One might think you had seen me yawn. I enjoyed every minute of it."

"Well, Ted, don't you see: we have got tons of money, haven't we?"

"I don't know about tons, but we've got enough to be going on with."

She tripped over to her dressing-table, did something to her face, played the xylophone on some ivory boxes, nervously patted her hair, and then resolutely resumed:

"Ted, I think it's absolutely your duty to do something for Mr. Gudgeon. You simply *must* give him a chance with a London theatre."

"How much would it cost?" asked Grunt.

"Oh, *I* don't know. What's the good of being a man if you don't know that?" exclaimed Mrs. Grunt impatiently.

"Sorry, darling," said Edward Grunt: "he's damned good and I'll see he gets a fair show somehow."

"Thank you, darling," said she; and then, after he had solemnly kissed her and was vanishing, in a matter-of-fact way, through the communicating door, she raised her voice:

"Do come in to me, darling, if you'd like to. I didn't mean it just now, really. I'd like you to!"

*   *   *   *

Thus began the career of Stanley Gudgeon. The Grunts took a theatre for him. It has often been done for people better, or no worse. As a rule the venture, begun with such high hopes, such faith, such assurance of infinite backing, such confidence of judgment, such supercilious finesse of casting, such pathetic certainty of giving the metropolis a new direction, crashes in a month. A silly play is rapidly chosen: a cast full of mouldering names is engaged; all the engines of publicity are set in motion; posters appear on all the buses; and, after a week or two of newspaper contumely and public indifference, the last ripple dies at the edges of the pond and all is as if it had never been. But there are rare exceptions, and Gudgeon's enterprise was one. Backed by the money of the Grunts, he took a theatre; uncertain as to which of three Lithuanian plays to put on, he found himself, one Sunday night, at a performance of the Arts Theatre Club. There did he witness an old-fashioned farce, patently modelled on *Charley's Aunt*. He loathed it, or, rather, was utterly bored by it, himself; but he had the instinct for success, and that permitted him to notice that an extremely mixed audience rolled about throughout the play, laughed till it cried, and tottered out, at eleven o'clock, both laughing and crying. He fixed up with the author, behind the scenes, and on very advantageous terms, that very night. The play is running still. Where did we begin? Wasn't it here that we began? Yes, it was: Stanley Gudgeon, a power in the theatrical world, had made his pile. He was running five theatres, all with modern comedies, and now had to get right with the spirit of Ibsen. So he advertised for a poetic play. So he was sent hundreds. So he chose one. So he put one on. So here the latter portion of this sad story begins.

*　　　*　　　*　　　*

Stanley Gudgeon yielded to no man in his opinion of his own opinion. But once you have bought a coat with an Astrakhan collar, you feel that it is your plain duty to delegate everything that can be delegated. He had, for his blank-verse play competition, a Reading Committee.

"Of course," said he to various friends whom he met at his various clubs, and to aspiring authors, and to aspiring actors, "I can hardly be expected to weed out the rubbish myself. I have a lot of very clever young people to do that. But the final choice will, of course, be made by myself."

So able had he been in his manipulation of the finances of the company, that he was really no longer at all under the power of those rather pathetic provincials in North (or it may be South) Shields: but he was not one of those who kick down the ladder up which they have climbed, and he did ask Mrs. Grunt to sit on the Committee of Judges, his Selection Committee. With her were a poet, officially accredited by a knighthood, and a dramatic critic, unofficially accredited because no paper coming out more frequently than once a week would employ him. The dramatic critic never turned up (though he took his cheque) at the meetings of the Selection Committee. The poet and Mrs. Grunt did it all by themselves.

They were tempted by a hundred and twenty plays about King Arthur. They saw merits in a hundred and nineteen plays about Tristram and Iseult. They hankered after a hundred and eighteen plays about Helen of Troy. They rejected, with reluctance, a hundred and seventeen plays about Faust. In the end, reluctantly but inevitably, they agreed that the obvious and inevitable winner was a play, by one Rupert Slater, called *A Stain on the Shield*. It was gruesome, perhaps; and there might be some things in it which would make censor and audience wince; but it was undoubtedly the best of the plays submitted.

One says they were tempted by all the others. "They" might be better represented by "She." The conferences took place at a dozen lunches at the Verbena restaurant. The poet turned up every time drunk, jovially indifferent and late; Mrs. Grunt turned up early, eager, well-shingled in body and soul; excited at this chance of starting an epoch in the London theatre. When she had doubts the poet echoed them; when she was enthusiastic so was he; he had been paid his fee and he was very pessimistic about the works of everybody except himself. When, at the last luncheon, she said to him, fire in her eyes: "Well, Sir William, I *can* tell Mr. Gudgeon, can't I, that we agree about this play?" he replied, with muzzy emphasis: "I *can't* tell you how strongly I agree with you. I couldn't help thinking all the time that that must be our choice;" and, he added, looking her in the eyes earnestly, "I knew you'd think so, too."

A quiver went through her. Why hadn't she met poets when she was younger? But, though he had passed it all off very well, he had never read one line of one manuscript. However, he had appreciated the lobster and the Burgundy.

*   *   *   *

The announcement was made. The £1,000 prize had been awarded to Mr. Rupert Slater for *A Stain on the Shield*; the première (a word never used of vulgarly popular plays) was to take place two months hence: would Mr. Slater (who had given no address) please come and see Mr. Gudgeon at the Marchioness Theatre.

Mr. Slater came: he saw Mr. Gudgeon and was duly deferential. He was a crinkly-haired young man who appeared, even at his early age, to have seen better days.

"It's been the devil and all to get through," said he.

Stanley Gudgeon diagnosed genius in struggle where a less percipient person might merely have guessed at drink. There was a little talk about casting: Mr. Slater, refreshingly different from the majority of these ignorant but exacting authors, was extraordinarily anxious to leave "all the technical side" to Mr. Gudgeon. So moved was Gudgeon by this tribute from a man of letters, that he at once rang for his secretary, had the cheque for a thousand pounds made out, and presented it to the grateful author. Mr. Rupert Slater was touchingly overcome by emotion.

"O' man," he faltered, "I don' know wha' to say. It'sh qui' a surprish, ye know. Well, take it I shan't forgesh;" and grasping the cheque firmly in his right hand, he walked very vertically out of the room, pausing at the door for a low bow and a still lower whisking of the hat.

That was that. And now for the first night.

*   *   *   *

The first night came. So did Mr. Bernard Reckitt, Sir Oswald Plumtree, the Marquis and Marchioness (in separate parties) of Humbermouth, Mr. Willie

Osborne (with his usual monocle), Lady Ursula Stein, Lady Underdown, Sir Hubert Umfreville (that inveterate first-nighter), Miss Marjory Eckhard (full of news from the Lido), Miss Diana Porterhouse (whose father has just bought her a charming hunting-box at Melton Mowbray), that beautiful débutante, Miss Inge-Link, Lord Benger (who, though he has at last retired from the Bench, takes as keen an interest in affairs as ever), the Chancellor of the Duchy (taking a well-earned rest from his exacting official duties), Lord Peebles (whose news from the Jockey Club many people would give their eyes to hear), the Hon. Timothy Tibbs (who is an inveterate first-nighter), and that inveterate first-nighter, Sir Ezekiel Cohen. There were also present about a thousand persons, boxes, stalls, circle, pit, and gallery not commonly, or indeed ever, mentioned in the papers. And the whole lot rose as one man. They cheered after the first act. They cheered still more after the second act. At the end of the play they simply rose and roared, all restraint vanishing, all class-distinctions going by the board. Stanley Gudgeon had done it again. And he had done what nobody else had done. He had put on a blank-verse play by an unknown living author, which was so dramatic that it had entirely captivated a cynical London first-night audience.

The audience had certainly been swept off its feet. Not only had it enjoyed itself, but it had enjoyed itself at a play in verse, and an intellectual play at that: the experience was unique, and gratitude was consequently exuberant.

As the audience, so the Press. Every dramatic critic in London, even the most carping and cautious, even the most theoretically exacting, saluted this new author, who had at last done what nobody since the Elizabethans had done: written a play in verse which was so thumpingly dramatic that the gallery could enjoy it as much as the stalls.

One slight qualification there was. The critic of a twopenny daily, while very friendly, observed that "Mr. Slater would hardly have written his play in its present form, had he not been, to some extent (however slight), in the debt of Robert Browning, whom all too few people read nowadays." But this was only a very small fly in a very large piece of amber. The *Sentinel* said: "Masterpiece." The *Messenger* said: "It brings us back to the days of Ben Jonson, when blank verse was the natural speech of the man-in-the-street." The *Telegram* said: "Mr. Gudgeon is evidently one of those men for whom the word 'failure' is not in the dictionary; it has always been known that his ultimate object was to restore poetry to the stage; and now, without hesitation or fuss, he has done it, walking into the great succession 'as stars into their appointed places.'"

All London, temporarily tired of strained wit,

pyjamas, the conflict between callous youth and puzzled age, bedrooms, revolvers, chintzes, cocktails and Chinamen, flocked to the play. "This is new," everybody said: "this heralds a reaction."

And so it might have been. Nobody knows where a reaction may not come from next. But a fortnight after the play had first been put on, a humble critic on the *Theatrical and Athletic Weekly*, who had gone three times with pencil and notebook, and knew shorthand, being so impressed by the poetry of the play, happened to quote in his paper the following passage:

GRESHAM: Oh, to my chamber! When we meet there
    next we shall be friends.
      (*They bear out the body of* SETON)
    Will she die, Margaret?
MARGARET: Where are you taking me?
GRESHAM: He fell just here.
    Now answer me. Shall you in your whole life—
    You who have nought to do with Seton's fate,
    Not you have seen his breast upon the turf,
    Shall you e'er walk this way if you can help?
    When you and Geoffrey wander arm-in-arm
    Through our ancestral grounds, will not a shade
    Be ever on the meadow and the waste—
    Another kind of shade than when the night
    Shuts the woodside with all its whispers up?
    But will you ever so forget his breast

> As carelessly to cross this bloody turf
> Under the black yew avenue? That's well!
> You turn your head: and I then?—

MARGARET: What is done
> Is done. My care is for the living. Alan,
> Bear up against this burden: more remains
> To set the neck to.

This did Mr. James Lunn of that weekly paper quote: this did his son, a Freshman at St. Simeon's College, Cambridge, see—for he was a pious and unusual youth, and always read his father's writings. It was not very often that his father used the word "bloody," even in quotation: his father frequently, at home, denounced Mr. Bernard Shaw for having vulgarised the stage with the word, and still more frequently, in his favourite tavern, denounced Mr. Shaw for emasculating one of the few remaining words with which a man could blow off steam when things were almost beyond words. The phrase, thus, arrested the boy's attention: he then began uneasily to think that he had seen it before: he then remembered where: he then wrote to his father: and, next week his father (pretending that he had been leading up to it all the time) was allowed all the first four pages of his paper for his revelation that the play with which Mr. Stanley Gudgeon was drawing all London, was Robert Browning's *A Blot on the Scutcheon*, with the names altered.

Gudgeon heard the news five minutes before his secretary came to tell him that Mrs. Grunt was on the telephone, apparently in a state of great excitement. "Tell her I'm out," he said, "but tell her that, although you can't be quite sure, you think you heard me say something yesterday about lunching with her to-morrow. . . . No: tell her that I had to rush away, but especially instructed you to ask her to lunch to-morrow, as I'd something quite especially amusing to tell her."

*　　　*　　　*　　　*

The news hadn't yet reached the general public. The theatre was full. The audience was enthusiastic. The people in the box-office were as happy as kings. The ladies in the bar were saying, for the fifteenth time: "Well, I never! and poetry, too! but what I always say is that you never can tell in the theatre. Now I remember—you was there, too, wasn't you, Elsie—at that play, *The Cinema Girl* . . ."

Stanley Gudgeon, at the crisis of his career, was sitting in his little private room upstairs, surrounded by telephones, flowers, enormous fuzzy photographs of actresses, embossed note-paper and leather-padded chairs. He rang up the number of Mr. Rupert Slater: it was only a last resort, for he had tried it daily for weeks: the answer, as before, was "Mr. Slater left here a fortnight ago, and we believe that he has gone

c

abroad." He leaned his head upon his hands: and then, after five minutes, he had a brain-wave. He pressed the button to the house-exchange.

"Get me Park 11152," he said.

He waited. There came an answer, rather petulant, in Mrs. Grunt's voice.

"Is that Mrs. Grunt?" he asked. There was an answer. "This is Stanley Gudgeon, speaking." There was an answer. "Could you lunch with me to-morrow at the Savoy?" There was an answer. "No, please don't make up your mind before you've heard what I've got to say." There was an answer. "Yes, I do assure you I knew all the time: not only that, but I did it on purpose." There was an answer. "You see—and I know you've always agreed with me—I think it's disgusting the way these highbrows in the theatre always chase after the latest fashion. And I was determined to teach them a lesson. I put the play on without telling anyone. It was an awful wrench, but I felt that I had to put it on without even telling you." There was an answer.

He sank back into his chair, relieved. He wished Rupert Slater in hell. But then he pulled himself together. Dash it all, hadn't he really known all the time? He rang up a few friends on the Press and asked them to supper.

It all worked out according to plan. "Mr. Gudgeon's Exposure": "Mr. Gudgeon's Challenge": "Mr.

Gudgeon's Fearless Blow": "Mr. Gudgeon's Triumphant Risk." They all, let into the secret, honestly confessed (and why not?) that they had forgotten their Browning; and they all took their hats off to Mr. Gudgeon for so benevolently defrauding them. Rupert Slater, content with his thousand pounds, was forgotten: it was agreed that Mr. Stanley Gudgeon, the most brilliant *entrepreneur* who had honoured West End theatredom with his patronage since the war, had taught all his fellows a much-needed lesson. Mr. Gudgeon was a devotee of the classics; and from earliest youth his intention had been to bring the plays of Browning back to the stage.

*   *   *   *

It was twelve o'clock. They were drinking champagne together, having finished the oysters, at Bingo's.

"Stanley," said Mrs. Grunt earnestly, "I still don't think it was quite fair of you, considering it was Ted's money, to do a thing like that without telling me."

"Ethel," replied Mr. Gudgeon, casting an eye around the restaurant in search of the gossip-writers, "If you don't know, you ought to know that I'd tell you *before* anybody, before even Ted, if I could tell anybody at all. But I *was* determined when I first came to London (and you mustn't think I shall ever forget that I could never have come to London if it hadn't been for you) to show these damned pretentious Londoners up."

Her whole aspiring provincial soul rose in ecstatic assent. She could have thrown herself into his arms. However, there were people about. And she had a husband.

ENTIRELY IMAGINARY

ENTIRELY IMAGINARY

I

"NONE of the characters in this book is based upon any person known to the author": "the personages in this book are entirely imaginary." How often, sometimes even with the qualification "in whole or in part," do we not see such notes as those prefaced to modern novels! They do not always carry conviction, especially when the reader is well acquainted with persons unmistakably portrayed; but even when they are mendacious, they may help to avert libel in palpable cases, or disarm suspicion in more doubtful ones. And, mendacious or not, such announcement of course helps to give the impression that here at least is a really creative story-teller, a novelist who has no need to resort to the tricks of the mere photographer, since he has a brain which teems with lively populations of its own engendering.

Sometimes an author knows that he has copied from life. Sometimes he does not know it. And in one recent instance he had and had not and knew it and did not know. A puzzling remark? But listen!

II

Mr.—but here we are at once up against one of the difficulties in question—what am I going to call the novelist whose tribulations I am about to record? I cannot, for reasons which will presently be plain, give his real name. Were I to call him, say, Aldous Woodhouse, I should obviously be asking for trouble. Yet if I just put down the first name I think of—as it might be, Philip Bliss—how can I be certain that there is not a novelist of that name who will at once suspect innocence? I could, of course, go to the British Museum, and make sure. But if I did, I should probably find that there were several Philip Blisses who wrote novels; or, if not that, at least a Philip Biss, a Philip Bless and a Philip Bloss, which would be near enough to be disquieting. Besides, I really could not face a long search of that catalogue in that great musty rotunda of the Reading Room, where you cannot smoke and the smallest biscuit has to be eaten furtively. So I shall chance it, and call him Philip Bliss.

III

Philip Bliss had written three novels. The first was the usual thing: a description of his school and

undergraduate days—which was rather melo-
dramatised, but bore some relation to facts—coupled
with the account of sundry "adventures," and a
violent amour, which might easily (as he told himself)
have actually happened, though, in point of fact, they
did not. His second novel, written after he had been in
London for two years, working in the Civil Service
and dining out a little as a presentable and interesting
young man, had contained less of autobiography and
more of observation, less of hectic dream yet more of
true imagination. His third had compelled the critics
to admit that here was a coming author. Callowness
had gone; no longer was it evident that each character
must be somebody whom Philip personally and
intimately knew or largely conjectured from the
newspapers, for types were drawn. Something that
promised a general panoramic view of English
society, with the nature and weight of all its characteristic constituents clearly appraised, was being
approached. *The Daily Lantern* had said: "Here, if we
are not mistaken, is a novelist in the making." *The
Weekly Sentinel* had said: "Here, unless our judgment
is gravely at fault, is a novelist by vocation." *The
Monthly Review* had said: "Here, though we know the
fate that awaits prophets, is a shrewd observer of life
whose next book should place him in the very highest
class of living English novelists." Naturally, with
such encouragement, Philip Bliss did his level best

with his fourth book. He was thirty. He already despised the dreadful crudity of his twenties. "Experience" now came to him in such volumes that he knew he could never catch up with it. He was already on the verge of that pleasant and enlightened period of middle age in which every new person one meets falls at once into some category of persons already known in life or books, and behaves as we expect him to behave. He would soon be able to create a Cabinet Minister, a coquette, a hostess, a theatre proprietor, a charwoman or a cabman, who would be a clear-cut person and typical, without being deliberately based upon any one person whom Philip had actually met.

Over the fourth novel he took the extra trouble that his sympathetic critics asked him to take. He worked on it—for he had now thrown up the job in the Home Office—sedulously for two years, whether in the Bayswater flat or in the Jimsons' cottage near Rye, or in Lady Alberta's villa at Antibes. When he had finished it he was pleased with it. It gave, he flattered himself, such a picture, realistic but not cynical, of London Society fourteen years after the war, as none had yet made; and without a sign of the monomania which makes people think that their own little set is all London. One thing only worried him. He had taken only little bits of actual people for his characters, and felt comfortably assured that neither they nor anybody else would ever know it. How could Georgie ever conceivably guess that one of her house-parties had been the foundation of the great and rather scarifying party in chapter ten, since she had been turned into an old woman, her house from a mediæval manor into a Queen Anne one, her proclivities from Russian and frenzied into eighteenth century and cool? How could Lord Beehive guess that he was the original of the Labour statesman in the book, even though all the elements of his technique of boredom had been analysed, for his appearance and his ancestry had been completely altered, and his passion for sugar beet had been changed into a passion for Communism? No, his reputation as a creator was not in peril; and his models could be trusted to praise the caricatures of themselves without suspicion, and even to suppose that they were all sly digs at others to whom they objected. After all, there were several Labour Peers, who, considered in a dull superficial way, might well be held to resemble his own Labour Peer more closely than that droning Conservative, Beehive; and he could well imagine Beehive, whose mannerisms cried aloud for burlesque, coming up to him at one of those infernal political crushes and whispering: "Ha, ha, me boy, you've got Antheap to the life; pretty brutal, pretty brutal!" One thing, nevertheless, worried him. It was this: had he altered just one of the characters quite enough? There was just one man, Simpson, whom he had derived straight from life: a repulsive person who was carrying on two several intrigues with two of his friends' wives—or, at least, so Bliss shrewdly surmised.

This man, with his name changed to Brown, he had made a central character of the new book, and this situation, a central situation. Not only that, but, guessing where he was not sure, and dotting "i's" and crossing "t's" in a way which the facts known to him hardly justified, he undoubtedly added flavour to the book. Here, patently, was a case where identification would be fatal, so he set to work, after finishing his novel, to sink Simpson without trace.

Simpson was fair, pale, clean-shaven, short and thin. The man (Brown) in the book became emphatically dark, ruddy, moustached, tall and bulky. Simpson's voice was a squeak; in the book it became a bellow. Simpson was a man of private means, son of a cotton magnate; as Brown he migrated to the Stock Exchange. Simpson had been to a public school and a University; reincarnate, he had made his own way in the world after a secondary school at Southend. Simpson haunted the Ritz; Brown lunched daily (as did Bliss himself) at the Savoy Grill. Simpson had parents alive; Brown was an orphan. Simpson lived in a Mayfair flat; Brown was transported to a villa at Woking.

Very carefully, when reading his last proofs, Bliss toothcombed the Simpson-Brown chapters for tell-tale traits; at the end, with a smile of satisfaction, he decided that no human being could conceivably identify Brown as Simpson. The two characters now had nothing in common except general bumptiousness, general unpopularity, and the sordid intrigues. Mr. Bliss was pleased not only at having eliminated all risk of libel, but at having behaved as a gentleman should and avoided all cause of offence.

IV

The book appeared. It was universally praised, especially by those critics whom he knew personally, and by his publisher's reader, a very generous man. The *Daily Lantern* said: "Mr. Bliss has at last done what we always expected of him; he has indubitably arrived." The *Weekly Sentinel* observed: "We always knew that Mr. Bliss was capable of a masterpiece; he has now written it." The *Monthly Review* declared: "At one bound Mr. Bliss steps into the company of the great English novelists." The sales were immense and grew daily; in many shops, though one window was still entirely filled with the novels of Mr. J. B. Priestley, the other was adorned by equally imposing piles of Bliss, pyramids of Bliss, pagodas of Bliss, solid card-castles of Bliss. A thousand pounds on account was sent him by his grateful agent, now certain that he would be able, by dint of Bliss's efforts, to keep the couple of racehorses for which he had long hankered; and Bliss himself began to wonder whether the little house off Regent's Park wasn't rather cramped and Hill Street or Charles Street mightn't really be more comfortably near everything and everybody. After all, he had three thousand in the bank, and the book, if it went really well in America, was bound to bring him in another ten thousand. An agreeable little lease could be purchased; and in one of those cosy Mayfair cottages his present man and wife could still quite well do for him. How near the club, too; easy walking distance, a rubber always within reach on lonely evenings, and a tolerable dinner when the servants were out. Alnaschar's tray fell; the cottage in Mayfair is still a castle in Spain.

v

One morning, a month after the book had first appeared, and while it was still burning its way towards Land's End and John o' Groats like a prairie fire, Bliss was sitting upstairs in his drawing-room-cum-study, trying to work at a play, but really day-dreaming about holidays in the South of France, when his butler appeared, looking very harassed, with the announcement that there was a gentleman wanting to see him.

"Who is he, and what is his business?" asked Bliss.

The butler, red and perspiring, was obviously in difficulties.

"He said his name was Brown, sir, and that you'd know why he had come."

"But didn't you tell him that I was never in in the mornings, except by appointment?"

"Yes, sir, I did; and he pushed himself in and slammed the door behind him, and . . ."

"Well, Parker, and what?"

"Excuse me, sir, but he said that if I didn't show him up, he'd come up himself . . and he threatened me, sir."

Bliss had no idea what was up; but his heart, knowing what hearts often know when brains are slow, stood still, and then began painfully throbbing. Creditors, now, he had none; enemies he had striven not to make. Was this a lunatic, or a blackmailer with an awkward, though trumped-up, accusation up his sleeve? He simply couldn't guess. The more cowardly side of him urged him to send the butler down to face the music, and to lock the door; but pride indicated otherwise, and he said:

"Very well, Parker, show him up."

The door opened.

"Mr. Brown," said Parker.

There strode into the room, while the door closed again, an enormous man with a red face, a heavy cavalry moustache, and a body like a great bolster in a dark overcoat. He stopped and glared.

"*Well?*" he said, in a deep, sharp, sneering and rather nasal voice.

"I don't quite know what you mean," replied Bliss, frowning in bewilderment.

"Ho! So you don't know what I mean! I've half a mind to wring your damn little neck for you!"

"I can't conceive what you're talking about," said Bliss, irritably. His right hand moved to the little table beside the fireplace. Yes, there was the stiletto. Normally it was used as a paper-knife, but . . .

"Drop that!" snapped the stranger, whipping a revolver out of his pocket and pointing it at him. The dagger rattled to the floor.

"Now, look here, you dirty little squirt," observed the visitor, striding up to Bliss with outshot under-lip and clenched fists—Bliss retiring until the fireplace prevented further retirement—"What the bloody hell d'you mean by it? That's all I want to know; what the hell d'you think you're up to?"

Bliss looked at him in bewilderment. "I can't imagine what you're talking about," he said; "I've never seen you in my life before. You must be mistaking me for somebody else."

"You filthy little swine," remarked the stranger, "d'you really think you're going to get away with that? I suppose you're not Mr. Philip bloody Bliss! I suppose you didn't write this god-damned silly novel I've got here!" And he drew from his pocket a copy of *Quartette* and thumped it on a small table, which was upset.

"Of course I'm Philip Bliss," whimpered the novelist, "and of course I wrote the novel, but I don't see what on earth that has to do with you, or why you should come in here threatening me."

"Something better than threats, I fancy," sneered Mr. Brown. "What I want to know is why in the devil's name, you damned little pup, you wanted to put me and my affairs in your rotten pimping book!"

"But I've never even heard of you, much less seen you," complained Bliss.

"My God, you little viper, I've half a mind to strangle you!" replied the huge Brown, "and would too, if I didn't think there was a better way of getting at you. You've got the sauce to say that you've never seen me. I suppose you'll say you've never lunched at the Savoy Grill next!"

"I shouldn't," said Bliss, "for I go there almost every day."

"Thank God for one spot of truth, at any rate," said Brown; "and perhaps you may admit next that you've even seen me there, day after day, at the next table?"

"I certainly never have," replied the novelist.

"And you've never observed me there with Mrs.

Green and Mrs. Hargrave, whom you've got into trouble for no fault of their own?"

Bliss looked completely lost. "I simply," he said, "can't imagine what you're talking about."

"Oh, you can't, can't you?" remarked Brown. "And I suppose you can't imagine why a man should object to his name, appearance, voice, occupation, opinions and private amusements being put down in one of your filthy modern novels? You can't imagine how a Philistine like me ever happened to come across it all. You can't imagine why I should object. You can't imagine why my women friends should mind your crawling across them with your slime. You think you can do anything in this damned free-and-easy age. Well, Mr. bloody Bliss, you'll learn something to the contrary!" He shoved his face into the shrinking Bliss's, made as if to hit him, thought better of it, sourly smiled, took a flying and successful kick at an occasional table covered with glass and china ornaments, collected over long years, barged out of the room, stamped down the stairs, banged the front door, and vanished.

VI

"But," said Bliss to his solicitor, Mr. Prodger, "this writ is quite absurd. Really I never heard of this man in my life before."

The solicitor smiled warily, though sympathetically. "Don't you think, Mr. Bliss," he said, touching finger-tips, "you might be quite candid with me, as your father was one of my oldest friends?"

Bliss felt desperate. "But I *am* being quite candid with you," he said. "Honestly, my character was a pure invention. I didn't even know there was such a person as Mr. Brown."

"Do you expect a judge to believe that story?"

"I don't know what a judge will believe; but surely a judge, when an obviously honest man is before him, should be able to see that he is telling the truth?"

"Well," said Mr. Prodger, attempting with ill success to assume an air of complete belief, "of course if you assure me that this is so, I am bound to take your word. But I am quite certain that no judge ever could. You novelists sometimes talk about the long arm of coincidence, and I can only regret that you have been the victim of a longer arm than usual."

"But what can I do?" asked Bliss, pathetically.

"Pay up, I fear, Mr. Bliss."

"But how much?"

"Well," said Mr. Prodger, pursing his lips and raising his brows, "he's asking twenty thousand."

Bliss's mouth opened. "But it's awful," he gasped. "I haven't *got* twenty thousand."

Mr. Prodger did his best to be sympathetic. "These

things," he said, "are often settled out of court. I daresay if you offered ten thousand and suppression of the book, they might close."

They did.

How difficult life is, and how strewn with thorns the path of authorship!

But perhaps (if we must have a moral) Mr. Bliss was justly punished.

But perhaps (if we may be permitted another) it was very hard luck on him to bear the brunt of the counter-attack when so many others go scot-free.

And perhaps it was a bad idea to let duelling go out.

But perhaps the wrong person often got killed in a duel.

And perhaps things are so very complicated that there is no obvious manner of putting them all straight.

THE DEAD CERT

THE DEAD CERT

I

EVERY Wednesday night, from eight o'clock until closing time, Mr. William Pennyfeather was to be found sitting on a high stool at the counter in the Saloon Bar of "The Asparagus Tree." He had other ports of call in various quarters of London. But gradually, almost without intention, over a period of years, he had drifted into the one methodical habit of his life: at the same hour on the same day he was almost always to be found in the same public-house. All his haunts had this much in common: they were none of them very riotous, and they were none of them frigidly quiet. Even those which were in the middle of the glaring West End were tucked away up side streets and depended more on regular frequenters than on casual droppers-in. Otherwise they differed, their customers ranging from the auctioneers, solicitors, doctors and prosperous tradesmen of his favourite resort at Ealing, to the dockers and draymen with whom he consorted in the "Butchers' Arms" near the southern end of the Rotherhithe Tunnel. Geographically and socially, "The Asparagus Tree" split the

43

difference between these extremes: it was within five minutes of Waterloo Station, it had a Saloon Bar, and the tone of that aristocratic *enclave* was set by shabby-respectable members of the vaudeville and racing fraternities. The reader may have guessed by now that Mr. Pennyfeather was a student of mankind. If so, the reader has guessed right. He was even a professional student of mankind. His novels did not sell very well, but they kept him in comfortable celibacy: as all the reviewers said in unison once a year: "Whatever the changing fashions of the market, there is always room for the genuine novel of Cockney life, and no man knows his Londoners, with their irrepressible humour, indomitable courage, and racy idiom, better than the author of *Battersea Bill*."

Things, at eight o'clock, were quiet. Two cadaverous, shaggy and grubby actors, at the other end of the bar, were earnestly discussing something in voices at once husky and subdued. Mr. Pennyfeather, comfortably sheltered from the November night in stuffy warmth with a pipe and a pint, was talking to the landlord. The landlord had known him for two or three years, but probably did not know his name: this place was very unlike the "hotel" at Ealing, where not merely his name but his profession were known, and where he frequently played billiards with certain cronies. Here people were incurious: willing to enjoy a talk with a stranger and ask no questions, to develop a gradual semi-intimacy and still refrain from inquiry. They might, he thought, when he had left the bar, sometimes say to each other, "I wonder what that chap does: might be a lawyer's clerk, perhaps, or something to do with the railway." He could even hear Mr. Porter, the septuagenarian ex-bookmaker, shrewdly observing to his pals, "Shouldn't be surprised if 'e 'ad a bit of money of 'is own." Well, if he ever did achieve that desirable condition, it would be partly due to Mr. Porter, who had already appeared in three of his books under three different names, with many of his conversations reported as nearly verbatim as might be—for Mr. Pennyfeather was a realist, and could not invent conversations anything like as good as those which he overheard.

"Quiet, this evening!" remarked Mr. Pennyfeather.

"Oh, I dessay some of 'em 'll be in presently," replied the landlord.

At this moment he was called to the jug-and-bottle department by the tapping of a coin on wood; the swing door of the Saloon Bar groaned, and there entered Mr. Porter himself, beaming and buttonholed, with a grey soft hat and a new suit of checks: he was the Crœsus of "The Asparagus Tree," and a man who had three prosperous sons in the old business. "Took the Missus to the Zoo," he said, explaining his especial grandeur: then, to the dark minx of a barmaid who had suddenly appeared, "Guinness, me dear."

No one else had come in, Mr. Pennyfeather observed with satisfaction; there was a chance, therefore, that Mr. Porter might become confidential, which usually meant that he divulged deeds of peculiar rascality, with a jolly Falstaffian frankness that made his worst swindles appear the innocent pranks of a child. To-night, however, the sight of the two actors in the corner switched him in a more edifying direction. He jerked his thumb towards them, gave an upward fling of his head, and whispered: "Pore devils, ruinin' theirselves."

"How?" asked Pennyfeather.

"Bettin', o' course. Lot o' babies, that's what they are. Comes 'ere for tips—from each other! Hinside hinformation!"

"Stupid, isn't it?"

"Yes. But there, we're all of us mugs sometimes. W'y, on'y larst ycar I'll be jiggered if 1 didn't back a 'orse meself on a tip I got 'ere."

"What made you do it?"

"Off me chump, I s'pose. Just like the rest of 'em, when it came to the point! Said to meself, 'Nah this one *is* all right.' Jockey it come from; at least, he used to be. Little Dicky 'Arris. Come in 'ere with 'is precious tip, an' I went an' believed 'im. 'Orse called Absalom. Down at the first 'urdle. Come in last!"

"But you've always been so funny about jockeys' tips."

"Don't rub it in. I'm a mug, that's what I am. I thought this was different. You see, this little Dicky Harris—believe it or not—he's straight."

The dramatic revelation of this eccentricity demanded another couple of drinks. The calamity was shelved, and Mr. Porter entered on a long story of how he had suborned, and for some years virtually employed, several police constables, and finally a sergeant, to protect his street betting operations. With a sigh over the fallibility of human nature, he took a deep draught, then looked round the room, which had been filling up. "Why, blimey!" he exclaimed, with pleasure on his face, "if there isn't the very little chap that I was talkin' about!"

"D'you mean the sergeant?" inquired Pennyfeather.

"Garn, that old skunk?" frowned Mr. Porter. "No! it's Dicky 'Arris, the little boy from Epsom. Dicky!" he called; and there stepped towards them a minute horsy man, with very sharp features but an agreeable smile, a blue-eyed, sunburnt, wrinkled man with white eyelashes, like an unsophisticated and even kindly weasel.

" 'Allo, Dicky! 'aven't seen you for months!" Mr. Porter cheerily greeted him. "Pint, please, me dear." Then, nudging each companion with an elbow, " 'Ow's Absalom? Near broke me over that, you did, you villain!"

Little Harris threw back his head in mock weariness. Then he spoke, in a Cockney thick beyond phonetic rendering.

"Cheese it, Mr. Porter! D'you know, sir, 'e's bin raggin' me about thet there 'orse for twelve munce."

"Dead cert?" inquired Pennyfeather, with a knowing twinkle.

"Lumme! I can see you know all abaht it. All the sime, I give 'im some good 'uns in me time, and 'e knows it."

"So you 'ave, Dicky, so you 'ave," admitted Mr. Porter. His eyes wandered; he caught sight of some friends, and with a hearty apology he left the novelist and the jockey together.

Mr. Pennyfeather liked Dicky Harris's face, and before long he liked Dicky Harris himself, very much. It wasn't long before the little man pulled out of his inside coat pocket a picture of a trim wife and a healthy baby, and it wasn't much longer before he was pouring out, to the most sympathetic listener he had ever met, the story of his life. He was forty, and, until recently, had been a jockey—at one time particularly successful "over the sticks." Then, he said—and Pennyfeather looked down on a figure which was like the skeleton of a small rat—he had put on too much weight, and obtained a job around a training stable. "A bit of 'ard luck; boss give up": for three months he had been out of work, though another job was now promised. Meanwhile he had got into debt: that he hadn't saved anything, he accounted for by the disarming explanation, "But then, lumme, jockeys never do! Give a jockey the Benk of England, and it'll be gorn before you can wink." It would be different now he'd got a missus and a kid. But here he was, work beginning next week, he hadn't been able to keep up the instalments on his furniture—including a pianner which his missus's sister Mabel sometimes come in and played—and the men were arriving to fetch it away to-morrow. "Nice little 'ome it was, too!" He sighed.

Pennyfeather lit a fresh pipe, and looked around the bar. It had filled up: numerous picturesque characters were babbling in groups, Mr. Porter laughing lustily in the middle of one of them; but their own corner was still their own. He looked at the profile of the ex-jockey, who was gazing sadly at his own reflection in his tankard. "Poor plucky little sparrow!" he thought: then, clearing his throat awkwardly and trying to look nonchalant, he asked: "How much are they dunning you for?"

"Might as well be a thousand," was the gloomy and evasive reply.

"But what is it?"

"Ten pahnd, guv'nor."

The tide of impulse was now running strong. It came to Pennyfeather two or three times a year on odd occasions, and he had so regularly failed

to regret his wanton generosities, that he could
almost have budgeted so much a year for the
purchase of happiness by absurd prodigality.

"Look here, I say," he remarked, gazing earnestly
into the little man's eyes, "please don't take offence,
but couldn't I lend it to you?"

Harris gaped at the prodigy; and he went on:

"I can't bear to see a chap done down by such
rotten luck as this. It wouldn't in the least matter
when you paid it back."

"Thenks all the sime, mister," Harris mumbled,
"but I caunt tike it."

"But you simply must. Look here," hurriedly
fumbling under the counter, "here it is. It's nothing
at all to me. I've got tons."

He had his way. "My Gawd, sir, you're a peach!"
stammered the little man. For half a minute he was on
the verge of tears. Then he pulled himself together and
grinned. He refused another drink, saying candidly,
"I'm goin' 'ome before it burns a nole in me pocket."

He moved as to go, and then came back and put
his face very close to the novelist's. "Look 'ere, sir,
do you ever 'ave anythink on a 'orse?"

"Not often," replied Pennyfeather, with a gross
under-statement.

"Well, once in a way's enough," said Harris. "But
Mangel-Wurzel for the 3.30 to-morrow. It's all right.
Lad 'oo's ridin' 'er's a pal o' mine."

"Thanks for the tip," said Pennyfeather, "and good night, if you must be going. Your wife can cheer up now. I'm always here on Wednesday evenings, and I hope we shall meet again."

He resumed his original solitude. No, he did not bet "often." In youth he had tried four several infallible betting systems, and each one had left in his mind's eye a panorama of disastrous scenes, the last of which was himself receiving from a pawnbroker an inadequate sum for his grandfather's gold watch.

Conversation grew noisier, the passage of drinks was speeded up, friends began departing with affectionate salutations, there was a general welter of "Just one more!" "Well, goo' night, Tom!" "Goo' night, Bill!" "Till to-morrow, then!" "Goo' night," and smashing clean through this tissue of sound the landlord's blaring "Time now, gentlemen! Time, please, gentlemen! Long past time!"

He went out in the wet street, started out for his Tube station, and by the time he reached his lodgings in Paddington had completely forgotten, for he made no effort to remember, even the name of the horse for to-morrow, much less the time of the race.

II

Dicky Harris appeared in "The Asparagus Tree"

the very next Wednesday night. He peered round from the door, then rushed up, snatched Pennyfeather away from Mr. Porter (who had been talking about horse-doping) and began chattering eagerly in an undertone. He had only a few minutes, he said, having a train to Epsom to catch, but he couldn't miss a chance of seeing his benefactor.

"I 'ope you were On, sir!" he whispered.

"On?" inquired the benefactor, rather stupidly.

"Why, the filly, sir! Mangel-Wurzel. The tip I give you. Fifteen to one."

Pennyfeather blushed with shame, having now no option but to confess. He assumed an expression of exasperation at his own folly. "Ass that I was," he said. "I searched the papers for all I was worth in the morning, and I simply couldn't remember the name of the damned horse."

Harris was chapfallen to the point of misery.

"Fifteen to one!" he repeated. "Why, with only a fiver that 'ud a' bin seventy-five quid. Look 'ere, sir," he went on pathetically, "I won't give you no duds, I promise you I won't. I can tell yer when they're bahnd to win, and when they're almost bahnd to win." Pennyfeather, he said, could put his shirt on horses in the former category, and a modicum on the latter. "Friday, nah," said Harris, "it ain't quite what yer'd call a cert, but next door to it. One of our own 'orses. Ten bob wouldn't do you no 'arm, would it?"

Assured on this point, he made Pennyfeather promise, honour being involved, to take a chance on "Flibbertigibbet." (This horse, as it happened, fell at the last hurdle when leading.) Harris's tip had not been bad; but there you were, that was racing; and Pennyfeather, who had not the slightest intention of ever backing another horse for the rest of his life, congratulated himself on saving his ten shillings.

Harris, the following week, was full of apologies; it had been miles the best horse running, but the jockey was a fool.

"That's all right," observed Pennyfeather with easy sportsmanship, "one must take the rough with the smooth;" and he agreed to recoup his losses and a bit over by backing a runner in the four o'clock at Salisbury, twelve days later, this runner being in the cert class.

So it proved, and when he met his "Epsom Correspondent," he admitted with bold mendacity to having made nine pounds on the race. A wild thought even crossed his mind to clinch conviction by offering to dock his winnings from the ten-pound loan; but he realised at once how such a suggestion would wound his little friend.

Harris went away happy: one good turn had not only deserved but received another; and if he did not make his noble helper's fortune, he was no stable lad but a Dutchman.

During the next three months Harris appeared seven

E

times with seven tips—not to mention new photographs of his family, of his sister-in-law playing the piano, and of strings of cavalry galloping over the Downs. Of the seven horses five won and two lost; and Pennyfeather managed so to manipulate the amounts he alleged himself to have put on as to give the impression that he was winning very moderately. The only money that, so far as he was responsible, actually passed on these races was not his own.

One evening in February he happened to go, being engaged on a chapter in which a fast young clerk embezzled money, to one of his places, which was a billiard-saloon-cum-drinking-den at the back of Shaftesbury Avenue. Here, in his efforts to produce really free conversation from three young bucks, with whom he had made recent acquaintance, he consumed so many more whiskies than was his wont, that his own tongue became unloosed. Temporarily the experienced man-about-town, and speaking with the offhand air of one who Knew the Owner (in this case a chilled meat baronet), he impressed upon his young friends the necessity, if they wished to make their futures safe, of putting all they possessed on the tip that Dicky Harris had given him for the next day. In the morning, as he held his head over the desk which bore the half-written chapter about the wastrel clerk, he remembered his indiscretion and cursed himself for it: in the afternoon, when the evening

paper informed him that the disgusting animal had
crawled in last, he felt quite sick: and for weeks afterwards he took circuitous routes round Shaftesbury
Avenue.

Dicky's abject apologies after that occasion drew
from him a wry smile which bewildered Dicky. But
next week the run of success was resumed.

III

There came at last the week before the Grand
National, and with it the visitor from Epsom, who
had not been seen at "The Asparagus Tree" for three
weeks. The tavern was very full: the names of at least
twenty probable winners were excitedly handed about,
whilst a procession of anxious-looking men sought a
private word with Mr. Porter and others who were
supposed to be authorities.

Pennyfeather, watching the scene with amusement,
and occasionally catching an augur's wink from Mr.
Porter, had been wondering which of the twenty dead
certs would be Dicky's, when, with a hist-and-finger-
to-lip air, the little figure stole in at the door, stealthily
approached him, and took him to a plush-covered
bench in a far corner, as one who had momentous
tidings to communicate. He had.

Having fetched drinks, he opened, with an unprecedented solemnity of expression and a clenched right fist: "Have you got twenty pounds to play with, mister?"

For an instant Pennyfeather was chilled by the thought that more borrowing was proposed, but the phraseology, as the sentence was repeated, made the situation clear. A mammoth bet was going to be suggested; and doubtless on the Grand National. Well, it didn't matter: it wouldn't go on, anyhow.

"Yes, yes; I think I have," he said.

"That's the stuff!" resumed the Man on the Spot. "It's for next week's big race. I've got *the* absolute cert. Can't lose!"

"But," the novelist ventured, "isn't the National always uncertain? Can anybody ever know the winner of it beforehand?"

"Yus, and no; once in a while the thing's a cert, and this 'orse next week's a cert."

"What's its name?"

Harris looked around; then leaned forward, and putting his hand over his mouth hoarsely muttered "Absalom."

The name rang uneasily in Pennyfeather's head. Absalom? Absalom? Harris? Then he remembered, with amazement: it was the very tip the little man had given old Porter a year ago, and the esteemed Absalom had come in last. Fidelity was doubtless a fine quality, but Harris was, perhaps, carrying it too far.

"Didn't that horse," he inquired in a tentative way, "run last year?"

"Yus, boss, it did; come in nowhere. All the jockey's fault. Boss, you got to believe me. Took 'im hover the sticks meself larst week. 'E *cawn't* lose. 'E'll leave the rest standin'. S'welp me, bob, 'e's bahnd to! . . . An' nobody knows. Only the stible and the howner. Kep it dark—you'll get *any* price. Mister, never speak to me again if it's a wrong 'un this time."

Pennyfeather did not hesitate long. After all, it would cost nothing to humour the grateful little expert. "All right," said he, "I'll back him."

"For the twenty pahnds wot you promised?"

"I'll take your word for it."

"Boss, I'll put it on for you meself, if you like."

Pennyfeather hastily disclaimed any desire to give Mr. Harris trouble. As a matter of fact, he improvised; his few small commissions were always put through a West End firm of which a cousin was a director.

"Can you ring him up nah?" persisted Harris, touchingly determined that the glorious good thing should not be missed.

"Sheep as a lamb!" shot through Pennyfeather's brain. "I will," he declared with resolution; "there's always somebody there late." Then went to the telephone box behind the curtains, carefully closed the door, got his club number, asked the porter whether there were any letters for him, and returned with a thoroughly plausible rubbing of the hands. "So that's that," he observed with hearty finality. "What's yours?"

"Since it's to-night," replied Dicky, "I'll have a double Scotch . . . And here's to you, and here's," in a gleeful undertone, "to Absalom."

On the homeward bus he made up his mind that this must be the end of his career of kindly hypocrisy. Fake telephone calls were really too elaborate. He should have to announce his intention, when he next saw Dicky, of resting on his laurels.

IV

The week passed. Pennyfeather did a good deal of work, and contrived to bring into his book what he thought a satisfactory picture of a thoroughly innocent jockey; he worked so well, indeed, that he "cut out" most of his social life, and only once remembered the existence of the Grand National, then humorously thanking his stars that he was old enough not to risk his bank balance on anything with four legs. On the Wednesday, as he did once every six months or so, he took train to Guildford to have tea with a comfortable aunt. They fell to playing cribbage, and he stayed to early supper: by the time he reached Waterloo it was half-past nine, and dark, and the station almost deserted.

Turning over in his mind the scene of the country parlour, the old lady, the lamp, the woolwork, as possible material, he walked down the sloping roadway impatiently waving away a vaguely clamorous newsboy. Then he automatically turned left; and in five minutes reached the accustomed lights and din of "The Asparagus Tree." Pushing open the door against pressure, he found himself in a dense mob, and with difficulty struggled through to his accustomed corner. He shouted for a drink, then felt a clutch at his sleeve and, turning, saw beside him Dicky Harris, whose eyes gleamed with unusual excitement from a face preternaturally white and drawn. The small man gulped and then stammered: "Gawd forgive me, I thought you was off somewheres else and wasn't goin' to come to see me!" and then clutched at his hand and grasped it feverishly. "If only I could explain how unnecessary his anguish is!" thought Pennyfeather.

"Nonsense, Dicky!" he said, "we can none of us always win. I can afford to lose that twenty."

"Stroike me pink!" gasped Harris incredulously. "D'yer mean yer don't *know!*"

"What is it?" asked Pennyfeather weakly, the fear that he might have, hypothetically, won quite a large sum flashing across his mind.

"Why, you've won!" shouted Harris, forgetting his habitual secrecy so entirely that half the crowd turned round and craned its necks to see who had won what.

"By Gad, I'm grateful to you," cried Pennyfeather, with fine aplomb, slapping the other on the shoulder. "What was the price?"

"Well, I'm damned!" said Dicky slowly, his eyes blazing, his face wrinkled in a rigid smile. "To be on a 'undred to one 'orse an' not know it! Yer've won two thousand bloomin' quid!"

The figure was staggering. Pennyfeather felt faint; then he was aghast as the clamour swelled around him and finally cheer after cheer broke out. Half those present knew him; the other half were resolved to be in on anything good that was going. "Hip! Hip! Hip!" they yelled, and the nearest swarmed round him, cramming him painfully against the bar, and fought for the privilege of wringing him by the hand, forearm or biccps. He was completely dazed; and scarcely conscious of what was happening, when "Silence! Silence!" rose above the tumult in the voice of Mr. Porter, which had roared the odds on the Epsom Hill for forty years. Mr. Porter had mounted a chair.

"Silence! Silence!" repeated Mr. Porter. "Give the gentleman a chance."

Silence was secured. People from the street were gaping through every crevice and every unfrosted patch of glass; the landlord, the august landlady with her golden chignon, the little barmaid with a look in her eyes that offered Mr. Pennyfeather a lifelong devotion, were clustered in front of the hero.

"We are all delighted," proceeded the aged rascal, "that our friend Mr.—er—our old friend has had such a stroke of good luck, and 'as honoured us with 'is presence 'ere to-night." (Loud cheers.) "I know our old friend well enough to know that 'e's a real sports-man and one of the best." (Loud cheers.) "Sir," as he raised his glass in the air, "your 'ealth and many of 'em!"

The cheering was terrific. Great roars of it now came from even the remotest of the more plebeian compartments in the background. Then the ham-like hand of Mr. Porter commanded silence again. There was a pause of agony. Mr. Pennyfeather realised that he was expected to reply. No; there was no way out. He had to play the man. He set his jaw and stared at Mr. Porter.

"Mr. Porter," he said, in a voice that sounded very remote to himself, "I thank you all very much and I hope that everybody present will take a drink with me!"

There was a new outbreak of hurrahing, mingled with mild cat-calling. Somebody far away started the National Anthem on a mouth organ; the whole con-course took it up with great enthusiasm and in several keys. While the ovation was at its height, the landlord leant across the bar and took hold of his coat.

"Champagne, sir?" he asked hoarsely.

"Of course," said Mr. Pennyfeather, with patrician calm.

They didn't all drink champagne, but the gold-necked bottles arrived by the case, nevertheless. Feeling like a visitor from another planet, Mr. Pennyfeather stood in the centre of the pandemonium and waited patiently for time, pretending to drink with dozens of men, and occasionally clasping the overjoyed Dicky by the hand. . . .

Time came, and with it a beckoning from the landlord. In a back parlour he was presented with a bill, written with a blunt pencil, for £57 10s. 0d. He wrote a cheque, said good night, and passed, with a gruff greeting, through a crowd of his more proletarian admirers who still lingered around the darkened doorway.

Next day he rose gloomily and faced his loss. An idea came to him. He could recover some of it, at any rate, if he wrote the story down.

AN UNWRITTEN STORY

AN UNWRITTEN STORY

IT was the first time that Wilfrid Evans had ever been a member of a rather large house-party in a rather large house, although he had described many such parties in his novels. Competently, too: he was intelligent, well enough bred and well enough educated; and he had sufficient sense and imagination (he flattered himself) not to deduce a whole upper class from the occasional specimens whom he had met when some more enterprising, if not raffish, brother of his craft had taken him to a cocktail party in a mews, a semi-smart night club, or a late supper on the more elegant of the coasts of Bohemia. Some of these were eccentric, some of them had to scratch where they could for a living, some were disreputable. Some were *déclassés*, making the best of things, some were parvenus, painstakingly languid, arrogant and æsthetic, and some were merely amusing themselves by an occasional dive into the London of the snob-columns from a quite different plane. No: Wilfrid Evans was not deceived, and he was aware of his own percipience. He saw life steadily, he thought, and saw it whole: he missed very little indeed; and thoroughly agreed with kindly critics who commended his "eye for fine shades." Why enter into further details? He had at all events (as he frequently with some legitimate complacency told his friends) come to the conclusion that human nature and the distribution of good and bad were much the same in all classes, that nobody could be quite so vile as the aristocrats in Mr. Nokes's books, and nobody quite so epigrammatic as those in Mr. Stokes's. And, in the best quarters, his reputation was immeasurably superior to Nokes's or Stokes's. He continued, without having lived among the established rich, to describe their habits, conversations, loves, hates and surroundings in a manner which satisfied that intelligent minority amongst them, almost all women, who ever read novels at all. What did it matter that enemies sometimes accused him of a too deferential, not to say sentimental, attitude towards the prosperous? The wisest and subtlest of the dowagers, who had seen much, and remembered Mr. James, Mr. Meredith and even Mr. Jowett, were pleased with him. "A relief after all that rubbish!" they said: then looked him up in Burke, thinking that he was probably somebody's second cousin, and found that he was not. It was through the latest of his dowagers that he was now at Milstead.

She had written to him, with charming apologies ("perhaps you will forgive an old woman . . .") for the intrusion, a month after the publication of his last book, *The Poynings;* and his reply had led to an invitation to tea in John Street, Mayfair. He naturally went: the house was small, and the door was opened by a middle-aged maidservant, with long service clinging like an aura around her. He was shown upstairs into a tiny empty drawing-room and waited. There was a bookshelf full of good old literature, a few philosophic and religious books included, and a table on which were all the recent books of which anybody thought anything. He strayed awkwardly about, touching the dark Chippendale and the Dresden shepherdesses, and finally took to gazing at himself in a round convex Empire mirror, surmounted by gilt eagle and ball, studying with interest the shrewd, wrinkling eyes behind the horn-rimmed spectacles and the firm, rather ironic mouth under the little dark moustache. The door softly opened: he turned with a slight start; and there was a little old lady in black, thin and hook-nosed, but with cheeks that still had colour, eyes that still sparkled, and a voice which was girlishly silvery as it greeted him. Soon he almost forgot that she was not really a young woman, so quick was she, so sensitive, so keenly interested in everything contemporary, so gaily humorous, so pleasantly complimentary to himself. Afterwards a candid friend told him that it was the art born of long experience that enabled her, over the tea-cups, to draw him into so candid and even eager an account of himself and his hopes; but at the time it was as though two minds and two hearts were fully opening, quickened by each other, for the first time. Then, at last, there came a knock at the door, momentarily annoying. He cursed silently, and felt himself closing up.

"Lady Hunter," said the maid.

"Elizabeth!" said the dowager: "Mr. Evans, my niece Elizabeth."

It did not take long for Evans's annoyance to pass. Lady Hunter had not her aunt's wide cultivation, and would never move with such certainty. But her instincts were fine, though she was diffident and flushed easily, at first because of the occasional exposure of her lack of information and slowness to take allusions, and then, as the triangular talk warmed up and Evans was tempted to an eager fluency, from pleasure at his whimsicality or at the reflection of thoughts she had known but never formulated.

"What a charming woman!" he thought to himself as he walked away from the house, "and how well we got on": recovering the picture of her tall, graceful figure, her neat, light-brown hair, and straight features, direct grey eyes and swift smile: her modesty, responsiveness, and fundamental gravity which at moments seemed even tinged with sadness. "I am sentimentalising her," he said to himself: "she is a healthy countrywoman of forty, who looks less because an easy pheasant-shooting husband gives her everything she wants. Novelists ought to be more detached and keep their eyes fixed on things as they are!"

Three months afterwards, when the old lady had twice taken him to lunch with Elizabeth Hunter and the very ornithological and very kindly Sir Francis in Bryanston Square, he was asked down to Milstead for a week-end. "My aunt," wrote Lady Hunter, "says that you won't mind our asking you, and we feel that we really know you quite well through your books. I'm afraid that you won't find any material for further stories in our humdrum household: perhaps you'll enliven us by telling us one after dinner." He was to meet (for the list was given, save that several young women were not individually specified) a number of delightful people, whose dignities ranged from the Marquessate of the Glasspools to the captaincy of a certain Geoffrey Poole.

So there he was at Milstead, a house full of rugs, skins and heads, the first down for dinner, standing in front of a great stone Tudor fireplace endeavouring to sort out in his mind the names and faces of sixteen strangers, whose cars had intermittently swept up through the autumn twilight; half of whom he had never heard of before, though they all, old and young, evidently knew each other extremely well. Echoes of many scraps of greeting and conversation rang softly in his head: "Diana!" "Mary!" "We both liked your

F

last novel so much!" "Geoffrey, you're a perfect scandal!" "Such a good speech, I thought!" "It'll be another month before the leaf's off properly." "No, there's a new master, Bill couldn't afford it any longer." "I do so hope you'll finish another novel soon." "Dolly!" "Peggy!" He could quite well invent such a mixture of flimsy remarks; he had, in fact, often done so: they were natural, indeed inevitable. But it was one thing to describe a milieu and invent personages who resembled those who existed, and another to invade the milieu and guess at the relations of a number of actual individuals. The world of his novels was like this world; but which of his characters did these particular people resemble? In the world of his novels painful things were hushed up, and deplorable things were known within a certain small society and remained a complete secret to the population at large. He had heard to-day a girl in low tones saying something to another about "Booby and Edith." Who was Booby? Who was Edith? For that matter, who were Pinky, Foxy, the Badger and Pumps, to whom he had also heard reference made? This actual small nation of people was as removed from him as Sweden or the Argentine, so far as knowledge of personal characters and ties was concerned. It was not his society, and he had, he told himself with a little pride, no ambition to step into it, preferring his homelier club and the conversation of one or two people at a time, people with his own tastes and familiar with his own surroundings. But here he was, and he should certainly keep his end up: he was not very shy and not immoderately humble; he would, he knew well, come through without clumsiness.

With Sir Francis he had felt thoroughly familiar from the first: the friendly old country baronet with a hobby, might have walked straight out of one of his own books. And, after all, there were one or two rather striking and attractive faces among the others, which should make the visit worth while. There was, for instance, the lean, deep-socketed, sunburnt, intelligent face of Captain Poole: he was curious about that man: if he saw him a few times, they would probably become friends. There were marks of suffering, he thought, in that face: then, as his habit was, he pulled himself together and reminded himself that effects could also be produced by late nights or malaria.

II

Food and wine had come and gone: they had been served with fruit and the port was going round. Evans, seated three from his hostess on the right, had kept going not so badly with his two ladies. His neighbour on the left, Mrs. Fitzgerald, plump, blonde and fifty, was easy: musical up to a point, an inveterate and not stupid theatre-goer who knew everybody, including all the senior littérateurs, and drew him, especially after three several wines, into an almost flirtatious exchange of mildly malicious gossip and criticism: nothing is so unifying as a joint, half-suppressed titter. The girl on his left was not so easy: she was twenty, looked with a dutiful profundity into his eyes as he tried her with subject after subject, was really roused when he mentioned hunting, but became a shade more tepid when it became evident that he knew no more about fox-hunting than a Zulu. However, she was obviously consoled by the knowledge that he was a celebrity of *some* sort, and had easy relief with a young, rounded, curly-haired, fair-moustached, jocular man on her left, who was patently an intimate.

Evans felt mellow and at his ease, as a conversation *à trois* between these two and a cleverish hard-looking girl, Diana Spurway, beyond, developed and left him for a moment free to listen, watch or lapse into brief reverie. The general babble grew dim, as he gazed at the light shining through his wine, at the long, polished table, the napery, the painted china, the shining silver, the shadowed shirts and faint-gleaming buttons of the men-servants, the curtains which shut out dark lawns, dark trees, an infinite mysterious countryside under the cold sparkle of the stars. The chatter returned and, unobserved by any, he discreetly allowed his eyes to roam from end to end of the table. Lord Glasspool's serious horse-like face with the small side-whiskers was half visible beyond Mrs. Fitzgerald, whom he was instructing in the economics of sugar-beet. Lady Hunter, cool to the gaze in a soft blue gown and a single pearl pendant, was talking with interest to Sir Michael Strode, one of the youngest and ablest diplomatists in the Service. Mrs. Bulfinch, a pleasant blonde American widow of forty in red, was vivaciously engaged with Captain Poole, Evans's immediate *vis-à-vis*. As Evans's eyes lingered on this pair, particularly on the mobile, expressive dark face of Poole, there was a light laugh from Lady Hunter at the end of the table. Poole shot a swift responsive glance towards her, and the thought flashed across the novelist's mind: "That soldier admires our hostess as much as I do!" Then he rapidly tried to fix the characters of the others: somebody's daughter, round, flaxen-haired, giggling, but shrewd; somebody's husband, fat, bald, clean-shaven, monocled, fifty-eight, also giggling, also shrewd; an elderly in-determinate spinster on his right; Colonel Fox, dark, hard, cynical, rather repellent. Beyond him, Lady Glasspool, an evident sock-knitter, was getting on very unaffectedly with dear old straightforward Sir Francis, with his untidy hair, twinkling eyes, ruddy complexion, dawning second chin and protuberant shirt-front. Sir Francis was doing all the talking: the subject, therefore, would certainly be the habits of birds. Between Sir Francis and Diana Spurway, hardly visible unless he craned his neck, were Strode's colourless wife and the far from colourless Lord Queenstown, a jovial Irish peer of seventy who had lost all his estates, had no money, and doubtless divided his time between his club and visits to the houses of old ladies whom he had known in the hunting-field in youth, and with whom he could now chuckle over ancient scandals. And then Diana Spurway. Brains, yes: but he had never seen so resolute a face in a young woman, and there was a tinge of bitterness in her expression which had struck him when they were first introduced, and which had even seemed to give a hidden vague irony to her first: "How d'you do?" . . .

They were varied, he thought; they oughtn't to make a bad audience for his story, if they really remembered to ask him for it; though it would probably be too subtle for most of them. . . .

"A penny for your thoughts!" whispered Mrs. Fitzgerald, roguishly in his ear.

He felt himself flush because of his unintentional rudeness, and said he wasn't thinking of anything— then, remembering that truth sometimes makes the most amusing conversation, corrected himself:

"No, that wasn't quite true: I was thinking of the characters of everybody round this table."

"Not mine, I hope?" laughed Mrs. Fitzgerald. "But I wonder how far you got them right. Character is destiny, you know, and you might be able to tell us something."

His powers of bearable repartee might have been unduly taxed, but at that moment Elizabeth Hunter rose and the ladies filed out of the room.

Sir Francis changed ends; the men closed up towards him; the decanters passed. Except that Lord Queenstown occasionally murmured a jocular aside to the fair young man, the conversation was monopolised by the three at the table's end; for Sir Francis, after an attempt on the birds of the Balkans had fallen rather flat, insisted in his bluff Englishman's manner on pumping Strode about the situation in the Near East. There was comedy in it for the listener: Sir Francis honestly trying to measure a hideously intricate situation with his few honest notions about fair play and foreigners, Sir Michael endeavouring to indicate the complications of the position without indicating the ignorance of his host, and Glasspool reducing everything to wool with a second-rate politician's cautious but sonorous platitudes. Evans caught gleams, now of quick interest, now of amusement, in the eyes of Geoffrey Poole, who, he gathered from a casual remark, had spent in the Near East his leaves from India; but the others seemed bored, and Colonel Fox flicked the ash from his cigar in a manner which suggested not only boredom but disdain—some of which Evans felt to be unreasonably directed towards himself. How he hated these conceited men! . . .

A last refusal of port, and they moved to join the ladies in the drawing-room.

III

In size and character it was more like an Elizabethan Hall, long, and warmed by two huge fireplaces in one wall. By the door was a billiard table, and yards had to be walked before they reached the comfortable end where the nine ladies, two of them already knitting, the others conversing in small groups, were scattered about on chairs and sofas. In the far left corner Evans noticed a great high-backed chair, dominating the assembly.

"Well," he thought, "if I am to tell them a story, that is where I should obviously sit."

There was dispersed conversation; Evans exchanged badinage with several of the ladies, condoled earnestly with Lord Queenstown about the state of Ireland, and asked Sir Michael for news of a personal friend of his own, who was Vice-Consul at a Roumanian port. He felt a little chagrin when, during a lull, he heard Sir Francis suggest bridge. But the ladies had not forgotten. Amid a chorus of feminine assent, Mrs. Bulfinch took the floor.

"No, Sir Francis," she said, "we're all agreed we'd like another form of entertainment to-night."

"As you like," he replied gallantly. "What is it? Forfeits?"

"No, Frank," came quietly from his wife, "we've a famous novelist here, and I've told Mr. Evans that if he only would, we'd all like him to tell us a story."

"Good idea!" said Lord Queenstown, Geoffrey Poole, and Mr. Fitzgerald.

"Admirable!" followed from Sir Michael.

"Rather!" said the fair young man.

Evans was aware of what he felt to be the sneering silence of Colonel Fox, and the yawning silence of Lord Glasspool; but, after all, he was not going to be cowed by men like those.

"Oh, please!" he stammered, with becoming modesty, "don't think I want to be professional at the week-end. Do play bridge; I'm sure everybody'd rather!"

This did not work, nor did a tentative effort to allege that he could not open his mouth in public—for Mrs. Bulfinch had heard him lecture "divinely" at a Woman's Club in Boston. With head diffidently bent he was led to the high-backed chair, while the elder ladies smiled complacently and the younger tittered with flattering excitement.

"Come and sit by me, Geoffrey," he heard Diana

Spurway say to Poole in that puzzlingly malevolent voice.

"I believe that girl's in love with that man," he thought: then, endeavouring to concentrate on his task, he surveyed the circle (Lord Glasspool was obviously preparing for immediate discreet slumber behind a brow-supporting hand), hemmed, and broke the oppressive newborn silence.

"I am not," he said smoothly, "a story-teller out of Arabia. I haven't a repertory. I can't, in talk, even tell one whole story with all its detail of circumstance. If I *must* bore you, it can only be by giving you the vaguest sketch of a story I'm thinking of now, which I suppose will be the next that I shall write."

The elderly indeterminate spinster spoke for once.

"Is it a sad story?" she asked.

"Not exactly," said Evans, smiling at her.

Peggy Strode joined in: "Is it about real people?"

"I should think not!" replied he indignantly. "This modern trick of pillorying real people, whether one's friends or acquaintances or strangers, in works of fiction, seems to me thoroughly disgusting and caddish. I'd rather stop writing than do it. For what this is worth I've certainly made it all up out of my own head."

"How lovely!" gushed Miss Strode. "And we shall hear it before anybody."

"S-sh, Peggy!" came from her knitting mother across the room.

Anyhow, that was attention: the studied indifference of Fox and the somnolence of Glasspool didn't matter with all the rest so eager; Lady Hunter all sweet encouragement, her husband all sturdy attention and admiration for a world beyond him, Geoffrey Poole so intelligent and so obviously friendly.

"You see," he went on, "I don't know how other people work; but for myself a situation comes into my head, and then a few main characters involved in it, and then the background and minor developments of the plot, most of which I know nothing about until I start writing. The result is that all I can do virtually is to tell you what the story is about."

There was a rustle, a match was struck, and silence returned.

"It's an odd thing," he resumed, "just at this moment, but it happens to be about a house-party and about a novelist reading a story to them after dinner."

"You rogue, you've made it all up!" said Mrs. Fitzgerald.

"That isn't fair; it really isn't," he went on, with a touch of warmth. "I don't get ideas as quickly as all that. This thing I first thought of ages ago, long before I ever dreamed of coming here. Well, it's like this—and though I don't want to boast," he laughed— "I must say I think it's rather ingenious.

"There's a country house—any kind of a house, Tudor or Georgian, or modern, it doesn't matter— and a week-end party. This novelist—who might be me, but I hope I'm not quite so simple as I mean *him* to be—is asked down not knowing a soul except his host and hostess, and not knowing the relations between any two or more members of the set into which he is accidentally drawn. Well, what I'm going to do is to make him tell a story which will apply to some of the people in the room. Everybody there will become gradually embarrassed as they realise this, only he will never realise it himself, having no clue whatever to the secret."

There was a pause as the party turned the notion over in their heads. Then, with determined curiosity, Miss Spurway's voice was heard:

"Haven't you thought out any details of the embarrassing story that he's going to tell?"

"Well," said the narrator, stroking his chin with his knuckle, "I have roughly, but only roughly. It's like this: you know how one frequently hears things one's never guessed at about people one's known for ages, and then finds that all sorts of others have known all about them all the time?"

"Yes," was the general murmur.

"It's obvious, of course; and there will be one thing my novelist unfortunately won't have heard about. There's going to be what they call a triangle."

"How thrilling!" came the hard voice of Diana Spurway, while something like: "What, one more?" seemed to come from Lord Queenstown.

Evans took no notice, and continued:

"Three people are involved, and a special point is that they're all nice."

Colonel Fox's eyebrows, he thought, suggested that there was a departure from life here.

"There are a husband and wife (let us say the host and hostess, for drama's sake, though it doesn't matter), and another man."

A log fell on the hearth with a thud. Lady Glasspool's needles clicked.

"The husband is kindly but older than his wife: she has an immense affection for him, but when she married him she was too young and mistook her admiration for him and liking for his decent company, for the real thing. The other man she will have known in youth, perhaps: then he will have gone out of her life for years; then he will have returned and they will have fallen hopelessly in love with one another, but will for the husband's sake run no risk of his finding this out. There may (though I haven't made up my mind) be a further complication with another woman, who is in love with the man. The novelist will innocently tell this story; but the whole party, except the husband, will know that it applies to these three people in the room, and they'll all know that all the others know, for it will have been whispered about for years."

Mrs. Bulfinch lit a cigarette, and then, with what seemed to Evans a rather ill-mannered endeavour (after being particularly pressing originally) to rob him of the chance of filling in his outlines, remarked heartily:

"So that's that! Quite a good plot!"

"Yes," drawled Colonel Fox, "thanks very much."

It was rather insulting, thought Evans, for these fools to suppose that he was capable of telling anything which might be awkward in mixed company. Happily help came.

"No, but do let him go on!" said Diana Spurway sweetly. "He must, mustn't he, Geoffrey?"

Poole's smile was set and cryptic. "Yes," he replied, "there are lots of things one wants to hear about."

"Yes, Geoffrey," came the even, bell-like voice of Lady Hunter; "but do get my embroidery from the morning-room first, and then Mr. Evans can go on."

Poole left the room; there was some talk in constrained undertones. Mrs. Bulfinch half began to speak to Evans and then checked herself. When the work had been brought and Elizabeth Hunter's head was bent over it, Evans took up his tale again.

"Now," he said, "as I've summarised it I daresay it sounds a pretty crude and simple tale. But I don't mean it to be that: there is to be some subtlety and grace about it. Neither the actual pair nor the

imaginary pair in my novelist's story are to be engaged
in a mere vulgar and deceitful intrigue."

"How are you going to manage that?" asked Sir
Francis with a genial laugh.

"Let me explain. What I mean is that for the
husband's sake (or, if you like, for honour's sake) they
refrain from what is called technically guilt."

"Doesn't sound like flesh and blood to me!" said Sir
Francis. "But go on, sir, go on."

There was a tense silence which was interrupted by
the level and deliberate tone of Strode, staring straight
at Evans:

"I think I understand."

"I know it may be difficult to make the notion
plausible," Evans answered, "but I am convinced that
there are, however rare they may be, some people
whose natures are so fine that they are able to split the
difference, as it were, between renunciation and
surrender. My couple may not even kiss each other;
or perhaps they may have just once when their first
certainty of each other's love forced them to utterance.
It will be frightfully hard for them, of course. It will be
all the harder for her because she has no children and
now no hope of any; for him because his youth is just
passing and he knows that he is dedicated to old and
lonely bachelordom, and is perpetually agonised by the
thought that if time could only be turned back, he
could so easily put things right. I do so hope you will

realise the sort of characters I mean them to be: both of them so very sensitive and scrupulous, and the husband such an absolutely perfect old dear that, after they have first compelled themselves to face the situation, they simply never even toy with the idea of letting him down—apart from everything else they know they'd be haunted ever afterwards if they did, but they don't really think of that. No; it's not easy. But they do get something out of it. Rather than part completely or do what they have decided to be degradingly furtive or unforgivably cruel, they will control themselves and make the best of such consolations as they can snatch."

"Do tell us what those might be!" said Diana Spurway.

Evans closed his eyes. "I can't tell exactly what my imaginary novelist would say. I haven't thought it out. But there'll be things like these. They'll be happy, when in company, to know that they're thinking the same thoughts about everything around them, and they'll occasionally catch each other's eyes and smile with understanding. They'll both know that if they're ever in difficulty or trouble there will be one absolutely safe comforter and confessor for them. They'll meet openly everywhere as friends, not caring what people say so long as they have no good grounds for saying it. And sometimes they'll have meetings alone, natural or stolen.

"I see them sometimes," he continued, aware that now he held his audience to an utter hush, "leaning over the parapet of a terrace, looking at the blue distance together, or walking in a wood together, saying nothing, needing to say nothing. And now and then they'll have quiet meals together in London, talking commonplace with the utmost intimacy. He'll be left happy, perhaps, with a bunch of violets, or even—for strength goes often with the most girlish sentiment—a handkerchief."

Evans heard Poole's voice, very gentle, as though it were expressing the common feeling of the audience: "And they never have more than that?"

"Yes," he replied, "I think they must have just a little more than that. I think that just once, when the man is staying with the others in the country, they must be stirred to an unusual pitch of emotion. Anything may do it: an event, such as his being ordered away somewhere, or some brutality of fate to one of them, or a mere accident such as the presence of a happy young pair of lovers, or even the influence of a serene moon." He paused, and spoke slowly and impressively, the artist sure of his spell: "They will both be restless, perhaps. Long after everybody has gone to bed, she will think she hears somebody outside, look from her window, and see his dark form against a balustrade, staring over the moon-mottled park with its motionless elms, and lawns, and sleeping

G

cattle; and, with her heart fluttering but her lips set, she will throw on wraps and steal down the great staircase, and open the door softly, and he will hear her feet brushing the stones, and see her pale face with a finger at her lip, and wait for her; and they'll stay there for an hour, cheek against cheek, clasping each other's hands."

Diana Spurway spoke: "I thought you said they were only to kiss once."

"What does it matter?" said Mrs. Fitzgerald impatiently. "This only makes twice."

"I call it rather a fatuous story, anyhow," commented Diana.

"Well," remarked the American lady emphatically, "I call it rather a *noble* story."

"Excellent! excellent!" droned Lord Glasspool, pretending to be awake.

"What do you think, Geoffrey?" Miss Spurway went on.

Poole appeared unconcerned. "It seems to me quite ordinary and possible, and I think Mr. Evans told it very well."

"Dare say! dare say!" was Sir Francis's remark as he rose, "though it sounds a bit complicated to me. But I never professed to understand the present generation."

Whisky, soda and glasses were remembered. Everybody stood up preparatory to retiring. The ladies gathered their work and their books, and good nights began to be exchanged. Lady Hunter, who had not spoken for a long time, stepped up to Evans and looked at him so closely that he was rather bewildered.

"I must thank you," she said, "for your charming story. It's pleasant to find an author," she added, with a little laugh, "who realises that there is a certain amount of delicacy and honour left in the world."

Evans blushed: he felt very highly complimented. She moved to the door. "Good night, everybody," she said; "I hope you'll sleep well, Mr. Evans. Good night, Geoffrey; don't read too long."

"Good night, Elizabeth. Rather not!" Poole joined Lord Queenstown and the fair young man in their session with the whisky.

Colonel Fox came up to Evans and scrutinised him keenly.

"D'you mind my asking," he enquired, "did you say your novelist man will never discover the howler he made after he has inflicted this dreadful evening on all these people, and even risked giving the show away?"

"Good Lord, no, sir!" replied Evans, surprised to find that this supercilious-looking man had been listening at all. "It would spoil the whole yarn if he discovered his bloomer."

"I see," said Fox. "And is the old husband to have the scales removed from his eyes?"

"Certainly not, and I don't see why he should. After all, he's a simple old thing who has never had the least suspicion of his wife, whom he adores and who is sweetness itself to him. Why, it would be quite tragic if I made my story end by breaking his heart!"

"Quite right," said Fox, "it would be. Good night to you."

*   *   *   *   *

Wilfrid Evans thoroughly enjoyed his week-end. His hostess and Geoffrey Poole were particularly kind to him, and Lord Queenstown seemed to relish his company immensely; while Sir Francis, who thought him "a very clever fella, though a bit odd," obviously liked him.

When Monday came Evans went away without suspecting anything.

Nor, happily, did Sir Francis suspect anything.

As for Sir Michael Strode, he went off to the Near East, sighing because involved problems did not always work out so easily.

THE MAN WHO KNEW BETTER

✓

THE MAN WHO KNEW BETTER

It was the fast train from King's Cross: first stop Melchester, where Verena Morrison was paying her annual visit to her uncle, the Canon, and the cheery houseful of cousins. She knew she would enjoy the change of scene and company and the temporary respite from work; and it seemed as though the holiday peace was to begin with the journey itself, for there was but a minute to go and she had the carriage to herself. She tucked her rug around her, arranged the pile of books beside her, and settled down on the assumption that she had already started.

She was wrong. Just as the final clamour of shouts and door-bangings was reverberating through the station, just as the long rows of seers-off and seens-off were screaming their last adjurations of "Well, good-bye again!" "See you soon!" "Have a good time!" "Give my love to mother!" and "Mind you give my love to Edie!" the carriage door was flung open and a large man in an ulster rushed in, followed by a per-spiring porter loaded with bags and packages. A few seconds' violent fussing, a scramble for change, a slam of the door: the porter had escaped with his life, and the train, whistling fiendishly, was off. Good-bye, London!

Verena picked up the top book from her pile and opened it; but beneath lowered eyelids she watched her fellow passenger, who for the time being appeared to be unaware of her existence. A great bolster of a man he was; one of that unusual type which is at once large, plump and restless. He turned his back on her and pulled down from the luggage rack a small dispatch case and a large brown suit-case which the porter had just laboriously placed there. These, with puffing and grunting, he laid upon the seat behind. First he opened the small case, peered into it, and clicked it shut again. Then he unstrapped and unlocked the large one, exposing to her maiden gaze a miscellany of linen and files of bottles, brushes and steel implements presumably accessory to the male toilet. This covert also was drawn blank, and recourse was had again to the dispatch case, whose shallow recesses this time yielded the presumable objects of the gentleman's search: two thickish books with their bindings carefully protected by brown-paper wrappings. More snappings and loud breathings: the cases reposed again on the rack, and the bolster-like gentleman, snug in his vast ulster, stowed himself, with some preliminary heavings, into the corner opposite her own. With a great puff which was as a last and summarising chord to his noisy piece, he lapsed into comparative quiet, put aside his hat and began to read his book.

Verena began to read her book also, but she could

not concentrate upon it very well: the specimen opposite her was too fascinating. Above his flabby great
frame was a flaccid moon-face adorned with horn-
rimmed spectacles. His eyes were puffy, his features,
under the tousled hay-coloured hair, were like half-
melted wax: the podginess of the nose, the looseness
of the mouth, and the vague outline of the chin or
chins, did but confirm an impression that might have
been made by a single glimpse of his large, white,
probably moist hands.

"Well-to-do," thought Verena to herself. "Couldn't
have made it, so must have been left it. Educated in
a way, but better if he hadn't been. Obstinate and
weak, cowardly and conceited. Yes, above all conceited: he'd fall to powder if he were ever stripped of
his pretensions to omniscience and omnipotence.
Lord, and I suppose he's somebody's husband! Anyhow, he's much too vain to bother about pestering a
mouse-coloured spinster like myself with conversation.
I wonder what book he's reading!"

She forgot him, and surrendered herself to the
subtleties of the story by Henry James that she
was reading, soon forgetting that there was anybody
else in the carriage with her, and only infrequently
remembering that she was in it herself. They had
been moving for perhaps twenty minutes, when she
heard an affectedly robust baritone "Brrumph!
Brrumph!" from opposite, and looked up to see him

blinking at her. One plump hand was on the strap of the window.

"D'you mind, Madam," he asked in an educated accent, with a "he-man's" heartiness, "if I pull the window up? I often get a touch of asthma."

"Oh, certainly," she replied, adding a studiously charming smile, as politeness cost nothing and, after all, her surmises about him were only surmises. And immediately, while he was in the very act of closing the window, she discovered that at least one of her conjectures was wrong. He broke into volubility.

"Why, how silly of me!" she realised; "any audience will do."

He began with a disquisition on asthma, freely larded with "Of course's," "I daresay you know's" and "I daresay you don't know's." The mention of certain eminent doctors reminded him of certain eminent persons of other kinds: as merchant princes, politicians, composers, actors and actresses, hotel proprietors and bishops. Reported conversations between himself and these dignitaries gave her, piece by piece, a good deal of information. His name, for instance, was Cyril Roberts; he had played the piano and given it up; he had entertained largely and given it up; he had been a churchwarden and given it up; he had frequented theatrical society and given it up; he had made conquests in the world of finance and given them up ; he had begun a tempting career in politics and given it up. In short, the whole planet had been at his feet and he had given it up, preferring a retired life of cultivated leisure.

Verena, being amused, not to say astonished, was a docile audience, chiming in with an encouraging "Yes" or an exclamatory "No!" whenever required. An eager smile suffused the flabby features; the lids of the protuberant pale eyes blinked rapidly behind their crystals, as he warmed to his great theme. Here, evidently, was someone who appreciated him at his full value: a good little girl who really recognised his authority. A few casual references to repartees which he had made to notable authors, whom he called Arthur and Tom, led him to bethink himself of literature, and he suddenly broke off with:

"I say, what's that book you're reading?"

She passed it over to him; he stared at the title page and pursed his lips in disapproval.

"It won't do, you know, it won't do. I know all about Harry James; I was reading him, I daresay, when you were still in the nursery. You must know as well as I do that it's all wind, all nonsense. Just a highbrow stunt, that's all it is. Couldn't tell a story to save his life. A little affected gang pretend to admire just because they know that nobody can understand half he wrote, and he didn't himself. I don't pretend," he went on, "to be the man in the street. But I understand the man in the street, and what I say is that he's perfectly right in preferring good straightforward stories like the one I've just finished."

"And what is that?" asked Verena, abandoning her book to the seat beside her.

"I'll tell you," he said, filling his pipe. "D'you mind if I smoke a pipe?"

"Of course not," she replied. "And perhaps you could give me a light for a cigarette."

"They lit and he began."

"Now the book I've just finished is by somebody— you can take it from me—whom I regard as one of the finest novelists now alive. No frills, no obscurities, none of your preaching: straight stories about human beings like you and me. Good English too. I mean Wilbram."

Miss Morrison gave a slight start. "George Wilbram?" she asked.

"Why, yes. I knew you must know his books. Now George, I submit, knows his business better than any of them. And this last one, *The Chestnut Lady*, is the best of the lot. Have you read it?"

"Several times," she said.

"Well, what d'you think of it, then?"

"I think that Mr. Wilbram has certainly done his best to write a good book."

He frowned impatiently. "There you are again," he said, "you people. Never willing to admire anything properly. I tell you George has done his best, and a very good best: he's succeeded. He's got the lot of them knocked into a cocked hat. Where's your crab? What's wrong with the book?"

"Don't think I'm attacking it," she exclaimed, with more vigour than she had hitherto shown. "I quite admit that there are some very good points in it. But it is full of weaknesses, too. For example, there's the construction."

"And what's wrong with that, pray?"

"For one thing, there are several threads to the plot which are left loose in the air; for another, the story takes much too long to get going; for another, the end is rushed—as though Mr. Wilbram had been forced to scamp it in order to get the book ready for the autumn market."

Mr. Roberts tipped his head back and beamed patronisingly.

"My dear young lady," he said, "when you've read as much as I have, and lived as much among authors as I have, you'll know that the construction of *The Chestnut Lady* is absolutely perfect. Why, that slow beginning and that quick end are the very making of the book! And as for the loose ends, life is full of 'em: that's exactly what George was after."

Miss Morrison's face lit up with an even intenser interest and curiosity. "Well," she said, "what about the weakness in the drawing of the characters? I know he does his best to skate over the difficulties, but characters have a way of coming to life, and it is painfully evident when they have to be forced to do things, to meet the necessities of the plot, which we know they simply wouldn't do."

"Come, come, come!" he said, flinging his head aside with a jerk which made his jowl quiver, and slapping his knee with a protesting paw, "you're picking holes for the sake of picking holes. I think I know something of human beings, and I say that there isn't a single character in the book who doesn't do what he or she was bound to do every time. Every time!" he repeated.

"I'm sure," she ventured, with a disarming meekness, "you know immensely more about life than I do, but I can't help having my own opinion, can I?" He nodded graciously. "And I must say it seems perfectly obvious to me that Mrs. Chetwynd would not, in view of all we've been told about her unselfishness and spirituality, have left Henry in the lurch; and it's really too much to ask one to swallow that rapid transition of Gregory from a bear into the most considerate of men."

"But——" he interrupted.

"Let me finish," she continued resolutely. "It's evident that Mr. Wilbram *imagined* a transition. But in life there would be some indications of the possible change, whereas in this book it isn't led up to at all, but just comes at one like an incredible thunderbolt."

"Very good, very good!" rejoined Mr. Roberts.

"And I expect that when I was your age I should have carped in the same way. But you're mistaken, I can assure you you're mistaken. When you've seen as much as I have, you'll know that nothing in a book can be more surprising than the things that happen in real life. I know from my own experience. Take myself: if you'd seen me ten years ago, you wouldn't have known me; I changed myself completely in an hour, and by a sheer effort of will. And I've lived long enough to be certain of this: anybody may do any surprising thing at any moment. No. George knows what he's about; he's a realist, that's what he is. You don't know Nature when you see it because you're not used to it."

"Perhaps you're right," she sighed. "I certainly hope you are, for poor Mr. Wilbram's sake. And I suppose you think that he writes good prose?"

"There's nobody living who writes better," he replied with easy authority. "I think I know prose when I see it."

"But do you think he ever gets the absolutely right word or image, as the really good writers do?"

The train rushed into a tunnel with a scream, and amid the roar and the rattle Verena tried to collect her thoughts. What would this man say next about this obviously second-rate though intelligent and industrious novelist? The lights had not worked; she could see the glow of his pipe bowl in the dark, brightening and fading; she guessed that he was preparing a finally salutary piece of enlightenment for her as he puffed.

When they shot into daylight again his protruding eyes were gleaming straight at her. He was ready with his summary. He wagged a slow confidential forefinger at her and began:

"You can take it from me that Georgie Wilbram's English—his friends call him Georgie—is *All Right*. I studied style in the old days and I know what I'm talking about. But I'll let you into one little secret about Georgie."

"Secret?" she exclaimed, with a touch of astonishment. "What on earth is it?"

"Oh, I don't mean what you mean. I shouldn't be surprised if Georgie had a few little secrets of that sort, like the next man. I've heard a thing or two, as a matter of fact, and one of the stories"—he chuckled reminiscently—"was pretty funny. Georgie's been a bit of a dog in his day; but that's all over now—at least, that's what all his friends think, though one can never be sure with a sly chap like that. One of those quiet ones. Still waters run deep. But it's never been a habit of mine to gossip about people. Live and let live is what I say, and I'd certainly never repeat anything unless I'd got all the evidence there was about it. No, it was about Georgie's books I was thinking. That's where the little secret is. He doesn't know that anybody's found it out yet. He thinks it's safe. But it'll be a fine jest when I let it out—and George is taken on the hop."

"Whatever do you mean?" Miss Morrison at this stage wore a frown of genuine bewilderment. "You don't suggest, do you, that he doesn't write his own books? I know it's said about all sorts of people, but surely you don't suggest it of Mr. Wilbram?"

"No, no, no, nothing like as bad as that! Georgie writes his own books right enough. No. It's just this"—he leant forward, goggling and whispering hoarsely as though a host of eavesdroppers were concealed underneath the seats—"George pinches all his plots!"

Verena Morrison was staggered. "Pinches his—— Do you really mean to say that Mr. Wilbram actually steals his plots from other writers?"

"I didn't say 'steals.' That's a hard word."

"You said what comes to the same thing. What do you mean? What foundation have you for it?" She was now on the verge of strong indignation, but checked expression of it. She was still curious as to how far this man would go.

"Now don't tell anybody, will you?"

She gulped out a "No!"

"You see, when it comes out I want it to be my own little discovery. Now old George is much too fly a bird to do anything that he thinks anybody might find

H

out. He doesn't rob shop-windows; he finds what he wants in the holes and corners. Old magazines, forgotten foreigners; or, if it's a big man, the works that nobody reads. Now take this book we've just been talking about, *The Chestnut Lady*. George has put a lot of his own into it, it goes without saying. But the plot isn't his, not the plot. That's where he's so clever. He can do everything else, but he can't invent plots; so he does the next best thing and looks for 'em where he knows he'll find 'em."

"And where," asked Miss Morrison, with a constraint which was lost upon the satisfied apocalyptic, "do you suggest that the plot of *The Chestnut Lady* was unearthed?"

"I don't 'suggest,'" said Mr. Roberts, "I know. I have proof. It comes from one of the small stories by Dickens that are always omitted from his Collected Editions."

"And what is the name of this mysterious story?"

"I forget it at the moment. I've got it on the tip of my tongue. No, I've forgotten it. But you can take it from me that what I say is all right—right as rain!"

"And suppose I said that you could take it from me that George Wilbram has never so much as read a single one of Dickens's short stories, obscure or otherwise?"

"What! Old George not read Dickens's short stories! Why, George has read everything, everything:

and I bet he's read all Dickens twenty times, if he's read it once!" The attitude was that of a benevolent schoolmaster towards a refractory child. But she thought she'd stick it out until she had wrung the sponge of his revelations dry.

"You haven't answered my question," she repeated. "I asked you what you would say if I told you—swore to you, if you like—that Mr. Wilbram had never read any of those stories. You're making very serious charges of plagiarism, you know. I rather think they're libellous. Please answer me!"

With an ineffable twinkle Mr. Cyril Roberts answered her: "What! Old George complain of libels? The quieter he can keep about it, the better he'll be pleased."

"But will you please," she insisted, with her fingers clutching and unclutching, "answer my question?"

"Why, yes, my dear young lady," he responded paternally. "I should say, to use a phrase that you'll find useful later on, that you cannot prove a negative!"

"In that case," said Verena loudly and very clearly, "you are a libeller and a liar, and I should be obliged if you would keep your further conversation to yourself."

Utterly amazed, he gaped at her, looking for a moment like a deflated frog. Then a red angry flood welled into his cheeks and he looked as though he were going to speak. Then he collected himself, grabbed his book, picked up his hat and crammed it on his head, and bowed over the familiar pages of Mr. Wilbram. After the first minute a sulky pseudo-strength came into the lower portions of his jaw.

Her rage gradually subsided. Amusement resumed its place. She began to consider the great boastful baby as a curious monster. She came near liking him even. For one weak moment she dallied with the idea of asking forgiveness for her outburst, and then gently explaining that she herself was George Wilbram and the author of *The Chestnut Lady*. But, after all, what would be the use? This one was past curing, past any learning of lessons.

For the rest of the journey not a word was spoken. At Melchester he hustled past her, scrambled out of the door and began shouting for a porter without so much as looking at her.

In bed that night she began to read the short stories of Charles Dickens and found much entertainment in them.

THE READER

THE READER

TENS of thousands of people a year use the British
Museum Reading Room. Of these many are casual
droppers-in who come once with a day ticket to look
up a few references, or who remember at rare intervals
that everything they want is there; and amongst these
there are persons of all ages and stations, even beautiful
young women and ruddy-faced, smartly-dressed young
men. But at the heart of the changing multitude there
is a large number of regular readers, who go there
day after day, year after year, sometimes for a whole
generation of years. Trade, occupation or hobby takes
them there: they look up pedigrees, or compile historical works which are published under other people's
names, or they are engaged on huge monographs
which they will never finish, or they are determined
to read everything that ever was published about the
Assyrian Empire, or they are interested in Arms and
Armour. Many of them appear as soon as the Museum
opens and stay until the time for darkening comes,
and the endless books are left to each other's company.
Some, poor dowdy women and white-bearded men
to whom silence and self-sufficiency have become
second nature, come and go, fetch their books, carry

them back, fetch more, return them, and shuffle away at the day's end to their unimaginable homes without ever speaking to or apparently seeing even their most habitual neighbours. Others are more observant and with time grow cordial, waiting each morning to greet with a smile the old acquaintance whose line of inquiry they may know, but whose name they never think of asking. Some make friends there: the silent aisles of that vast whispering room, with its tall tiers of book galleries and its long radiating spokes of black desks, pen-racks, tomes and bent heads, its shuffling students, its quiet ring of officials in the middle, its austerity, its gravity, its airs heavy with reminders of the passage of time and the incessant advance of all-obliterating death, have even led to honeymoons and country cottages.

In the years 1908 and 1909 I also was a settled inhabitant of that peaceful if slightly depressing place, familiar with the diffused, sober light and subdued swishes, rustles, scratches, thumps, footfalls, coughs and horny mumbles which are characteristic of it. I was young and engaged on a historical work, ingeniously, if too picturesquely, compiled from the writings of wiser and older men who had spent very much more time grubbing in museums, amongst the volumes of still more numerous predecessors, than I ever intended to spend. And, being young, and being also curious about the types and given to fanciful

conjectures about strangers, I wasted a good deal of
time observing those around me and sitting next me,
bending over the heavy volumes of catalogue, passing
to and fro, in and out of the swing doors. After a few
months I knew many by sight and some to speak to.
Of the oddities, the very tall, or fat, or dirty, or
cadaverous, or shaggy, or strangely dressed, I was
sure I knew the face of every one. Those with whom
I made friends were more ordinary.

There was a man of middle age, spectacled and
moustached, quietly and decently dressed, who for a
long time sat at K.13 desk, which was next to K.12,
always mine when I could get it. He always had a
heap of books of heraldry in front of him, and copied
names, dates and blazons very neatly into small exer-
cise books. He was shy and it took us a long time to
get beyond a nod at meeting and parting. But in the
end we fell into the habit of going out together and
talking until we reached the gates. Usually our talk
was about his subject, and he once told me a very
strange thing about the history of a very well-known
family. His name, if I ever knew it, I have forgotten.

A student whom I got to know better was an
Indian, a tall, rather good-looking, amber-skinned
Bengali, who had a pleasant smile, soft brown dream-
ing eyes, and a melodiously twittering voice, and who
spent his time mastering the dreariest kind of railway
economics. He came several times to my rooms, drank

coffee, ate bananas (his one ardent passion) and told me all about his family and home and hopes, and something about his opinions. I went once to dine with him in a Woburn Place boarding-house, full of spinsters, medical students, aspidistras, paper fans and assorted sauces. His name, if I could remember it, I should not be able to spell.

And there was an extraordinarily pleasant young woman. It began with my helping her lift one of those very bulky catalogues; it continued with my pretending to be looking for the very same obscure entry as herself, the most minor of Elizabethan poets. The coincidence was certainly remarkable; we couldn't help observing the fact when we next met in the passage; and one day we reached the steps together, and made such sympathetic remarks about the cease-lessly weaving and murmuring pigeons at the top of the steps, that we naturally went to the same shop for tea, and fairly sparkled with excitement over our favourite Elizabethan lyrics. This became almost a habit afterwards. Her name is neither here nor there.

There was also in the reading-room, almost every day, all that time, another man who looked rather ordinary. He was a neat little man, short and slight, in comfortable quiet clothes, looking like a very respectable Continental shopkeeper. Continental cer-tainly; there was something distinctly foreign about him. Not more than early middle-aged, he had gone bald early and his thin reddish-brown hair had receded to his temples. He had a moustache and a goatee, but the foreign appearance was chiefly given by the high cheek-bones and the little slanting slits of eyes. "Pig-like" is the first word that comes to hand; but it is wrong. There was nothing coarse about those eyes: they were intent and direct and occasionally there came into them a metallic twinkle of good-tempered mock-ery. He spoke to few: when he did speak it was with an easy courtesy.

This man, who had spent most of his life abroad, had been trained for the Bar. At the Museum, where he was the most regular of attendants, he read very persist-ently. His principal study was sociology, economic theory, and the philosophy of history; but he read good novels as well, and he occasionally perused, with apparent pleasure, volumes dealing with the shooting of game. Every evening, when his day's reading was over, he picked up his note-books and walked back to the rooms in Holborn, where he lived with his wife. Those who visited him there said that everything was extremely tidy and clean. The couple were poor, but not oppressively so; the allowance he received for prosecuting his studies and occasionally producing a small political paper, was, he said, ample for their needs, which were few.

Some years later, a friend of mine met him at an evening party in Geneva. It was a very voluble party, but the little man listened, without doing more than smile, the whole evening. My friend walked away with him, and remembered later that in six words, which seemed so boastful as to suggest that he was jesting, he precisely forecast his own destiny.

Later he emerged from a great turmoil in which myriads were butchered, to be virtual autocrat of a vast Empire. His reading of history stood him in good stead; and at intervals he enjoyed a little game shooting.

To-day his name is known, for execration or reverence, over the whole world. From end to end of Russia his portrait hangs, where once was the ikon, in millions of homes. His mausoleum stands in the Red Square at Moscow. Within it there is a glass coffin, and he lies embalmed in it looking just as he used to look in the Museum, just as quiet, though older and rather balder and a little more seamed. By day an endless file of worshipping peasants goes by the glass case and stares at the wonder of this dead man, who will be a legend for all the ages. Through the darkest and bitterest of nights silent uniformed sentries, with bayonets pointing aloft, stand at guard around the crystal coffin.

It was Vladimir Ulianoff. That is to say, Lenin.

What I regret is that all that time at the Museum I did not speak to him. I did not notice him. I did not even know he was there.

EDWIN AND ——

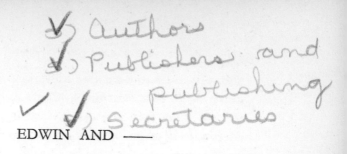

EDWIN AND ——

I

ARTHUR OLIVER, leaning gracefully against the mantelpiece, lit a cigarette and looked down at his brooding young friend, Edmund Thurlow, who sat in the large armchair, chin upon hands, hair ruffled, under-jaw protruding.

"Anybody might think," he said with an air at once compassionate and whimsical, "that I was asking you to give me a large sum of money."

"Wouldn't be much good doing that," mumbled Thurlow.

Then he rose, went to the window and looked down on the Embankment below. His clothes were not too new, and there was obstinacy in his pale, handsome, young face.

"My dear boy, *don't* be such an ass," resumed Oliver. "I thought you saw it all so clearly just now. Must I start all over again?"

Thurlow bit his lip and neither answered nor moved.

"Must I tell you for the fifty-fifth time that you're an absolute fool if you turn this chance down? Here have I got this great fat, bumbling fool Breeze to meet you, played his conceit like a fish and landed it, got him ready to print anything you care to send him, and pay you more than you ever earned in your life; and all you do is to go on biting your nails about it! It really is preposterous. *Do* be sensible."

Thurlow turned his head and looked him straight in the eyes.

"It's no good pretending you don't know what I feel, Arthur," he said. "The closer I come to the prospect of seeing my name in Breeze's filthy magazine, the more revolted I am. How would you like it if you'd made a reputation as a serious artist, and everybody who matters expected you to go on, and then you found yourself writing for the cheap magazines just to get money, knowing quite well that everybody who thinks anything of you will be disgusted?"

"Is it their disgust or their sneers that's worrying you?" asked Oliver.

"I don't care which it is," snapped the young genius.

"Look here, Edmund," said his friend soothingly, "I can see this business from the outside. Nobody is going to bother in the least where your stories appear, except a few dozen young shams in Paris, New York and the University towns; and even they will soon get used to the change, if you keep your integrity as a writer. Do as I tell you. Exploit this precious reputation you've got, make as much money as you can for a few years, and then go to Timbuctoo, or wherever you like, and write for an audience of five or six, if you want to."

"I promised I would, didn't I?"

"Yes; but if so, why on earth make such a song about it?"

"How can you be sure he'll print the wretched stuff when he gets it? I can't conceive that he'll like anything I can do, or he wouldn't print the muck he does."

"You really are too exasperating, Edmund," patiently repeated Oliver for about the tenth time. "I really did think you understood the position. I tell you once more and finally: The man thinks that what he doesn't know about literature isn't worth knowing; his conceit won't allow him to admit that inclusion in his wretched bundle of factory-made stories isn't a sort of seal of achievement; he's suddenly become aware that you are being talked about in all the world which he would and cannot penetrate, so affects to despise. I've encouraged his notion that you're '*the* coming man,' and I put the lid on it by casually, and quite kindly, remarking that though (between him and me) he was, of course, aware that you were about to leap into the most illustrious sort of fame, he would not dare—as an editor, in fact, he could not—print anything of your kind in a magazine which he, with such superb judgment, conducted for the half-educated public. I didn't quite use those last words, of course. I gave him no answer. But he so swelled up with enraged pride and almost ferocious determination that I feared apoplexy. Be commonly civil, Edmund, and you'll get a year's income out of one story."

Thurlow sighed. "Oh, very well," he said. "I suppose I can last out lunch."

"That's better," replied Oliver. "It's a quarter to one, and we'd better think of starting for the club. What about a glass of sherry first?"

They had a glass of sherry. As they were sipping it Oliver had one last after-thought.

"Look here, Edmund," he asked, with a touch of diffidence, "I take it that if he accepts a story from you and wants you to alter it slightly, you'll be reasonable, won't you?"

"Oh, I don't care," answered Thurlow. "I might as well go the whole hog."

"That's right! I'm sure you must see that no magazine with a wide circulation could be expected to print *some* of the things you've written. After all, a man can always say what he wants to in some other way—especially if he's so diabolically clever as you are."

The phrase pleased Thurlow—naturally. As he put on his overcoat he smiled and said:

"Don't bother about me. I'm all right."

II

The Editor of the *Cecil Magazine*, seated at his expensive sham Chippendale table, which was chastely adorned by a bowl of daffodils, a refined calendar, and a silver-framed photograph of his wife, gave the monthly figures a last glance and pursed his lips. The pursing was due to no anxiety, but was the mere symbol of professional acumen. Every successful business man, doctor or lawyer, mentioned in the stories published by the *Cecil Magazine*, pursed his lips whenever anybody was watching: Mr. Walter Breeze's face had been subdued to what it worked in.

Then he raised his head, and, with a hand on the arm of his chair, half turned to the little grey, clerkly man who stood at eager attention behind him, with a number of account books under his arm.

"As you say, Mr. Ham," he observed impressively, looking over his pince-nez, "we've all every reason to be satisfied with the sales, especially the company."

"Have you seen everything you want, sir?"

"Yes, thank you, Mr. Ham. Good morning. Good morning."

Mr. Ham and the ledgers retired. The door closed softly and Mr. Breeze was left alone with the refined furniture, the pile carpet, and his thoughts. He pursed his clean-shaven lips again. This time there was genuine reason for it. The round, batrachian face, usually held up with such self-satisfaction, wore a look of discontent, of sulkiness even.

What was the reason? Was there a tragedy in the background? Had Mr. Breeze's wife run away, or fallen ill, or (as the case might be) recovered? Had his son gone to the devil? Had he been gambling and did ruin threaten? Was he in fear of exposure by blackmailers or detection by the law? Was he in the throes of some great intellectual or moral convulsion? Not at all. All the major elements in his existence were, as he would have said, "as right as rain." His wife was precisely the type of beauty he admired, was at once decorative, efficient and economical; humoured his every whim and obviously regarded him as a very great man. His only son was but eleven years old, bright, spectacled and docile. He drew a large salary, saved a quarter of it every year, and invested his savings profitably. Nobody had ever found him out in anything discreditable; and as for his intellect and his soul, they had never given him trouble in his life. He had, he flattered himself, any amount of common sense and no sentiment. Nobody might have deduced either fact from the stories in the magazine which he edited. But it was, he might have explained, his common sense which led him to give his readers the nonsense they wanted. In terms, indeed, he would not even have admitted that it *was* nonsense. "Good healthy sentiment . . . Escape from the dullness of everyday life . . . Human touch . . . None of your sordid so-called realism . . ." Phrases like these came often into his speech when he was controverting with doubters or expounding to the sympathetic admirers who surrounded him on his suburban Sundays. But sentiment, whether healthy or otherwise, had never been detected in him by those who had worked under him or sought unprofitable favours from him. He judged his manuscripts by formulæ, and the formulæ worked.

Yet, indirectly, his intellect *was* concerned with his present unease. It had not been troubled by doubt, but it had been challenged. He had been boiling with just indignation for a week, at intervals, whenever he remembered the insufferable insolence of that damned patronising pup, Arthur Oliver. Who was Arthur Oliver? Pooh! nobody at all! What did he do? People at the club said he was by way of being an Oriental scholar. A fat lot that meant! Nothing to him at all; and yet what airs he put on! He could see the man now, with his tweeds and his low collar, and his orange-coloured tie, and his attitude, and his so-called good looks—affected brown skin and false smile, and eyes full of impertinent mockery. They said that Oliver floated about everywhere and knew every-body. Just the sort who would: he had "charm," no doubt. The mere thought of the word made Mr.

Breeze's mouth curl, as though he had tasted something sour: whenever he met any man with this so-called "charm," he always detested him. "Charm," he had once announced to Miss Firkins, his secretary, "is nothing more than another name for hypocrisy." Personally, he preferred people to be straightforward. He was, as he often reflected with pleasure, an Englishman.

Half-past twelve. In another half an hour he would be lunching with that swine, Oliver, and his so-called friend, young Thurlow. He didn't suppose the chap was a friend at all; why should a brilliant young novelist like this Edmund Thurlow make friends with Oliver? Much more likely that Oliver had curried favour with Thurlow by offering to put him in touch with important people. Anyhow, he would show Oliver that he had overreached himself when he airily assumed—or, more likely, maliciously pretended to assume—that the *Cecil* was not open to the best there was, wherever it came from. Yes, he'd show him. And probably this young Thurlow would realise at once, as soon as he met him, that here was somebody who had forgotten more about real fiction than Oliver had ever known.

Grey hat. Stick. Gloves. Passage. Bell. Lift. Page-boy. Taxi-cab. These objects passed before Mr. Breeze's eyes as he passed from his desk to the steps of the great office-block, but he barely perceived them.

His mind, all the way along the crowded Strand, was forming confused pictures of the coming luncheon party: in imagination he was leaning across the table, ignoring Oliver and talking impressively to Thurlow—Edmund Thurlow. He didn't, he was forced to realise, know many *details* about Thurlow: he was only vaguely conscious that he was one of these fellows who wrote obscurely, on purpose, and had a funny point of view, not quite normal. But he could scent coming success as well as anyone; and this, he kept on reiterating to himself, was the coming man, the coming man. The *Cecil:* that was the place for coming men: always had been. Why, two of his regular story-writers, hardly known when he started them, had actually been knighted. That was the sort of thing these Olivers burked. Anyhow, he'd damn well run Thurlow now, whatever he thought of his stories: Oliver wasn't going to get away with the idea that he was the only high and mighty one who knew what was doing in literature. And, whatever the difficulties, this Thurlow was going to be hitched to the car of the *Cecil,* or his name wasn't . . . The taxi-man had the door open.

"Arundel Club, sir," he announced cheerily.

With the air of a master of men Mr. Walter Breeze paid him and slowly mounted the steps. . . .

As he had resolved, so it was. He solicited from Thurlow a story, and it was all fixed up.

There were a few awkward moments *en route*. Oliver, while they were drinking soup, could not refrain from mentioning André Gide. Even Thurlow had the perception to see that Mr. Breeze might suspect that his leg was being pulled, and threw a quick, warning glance at their host. Happily Breeze took it that André Gide was the name of some French food, knowledge of which Oliver was trying to display. He grunted something about new-fangled foreign dishes and proceeded to demonstrate that he was nevertheless not without his tastes by ordering an omelette, a sole, and a bottle of sweet white wine— plain English food and no trimmings. Thenceforward Arthur Oliver behaved himself. Breeze was even surprised and gratified that he took a very small part in the conversation, contenting himself with a host's pains to put his guests at their ease with each other. Breeze noticed with approval that Oliver, who must have known that these were his special subjects, deli- cately dropped small encouraging remarks about the Hardy Country, the Brontë Country (Mr. Breeze came from Sheffield), the Phillpotts Country, the Caine Country, and R.L.S. With these congenial topics thus naturally arising he found it easy, between mouthfuls, to show young Thurlow how ripe the learning of an old littérateur could be. Thurlow, to be sure, had an odd way of listening: he kept on staring, almost gaping: still he listened, and very intently. He even, at last, invited information on a new subject: "What," he inquired, "do you really think of Shakespeare, Mr. Breeze?"—and Breeze was able to relate, very dogmatically and fluently, his impressions of the productions of Sir Henry Irving and Sir H. Beerbohm Tree.

Coffee they had in a corner of the smoking-room. Well padded and warmed by his brandy and the pleasing atmosphere of deference, the Editor proceeded to launch his benevolent thunderbolt.

"I have for a long time been thinking, Mr. Thurlow —ever since your first novel—er—that thing, you know, came out, in fact—of writing to ask you whether you wouldn't honour the *Cecil* with a story."

Thurlow, who had few of the social graces, mumbled a poor imitation of delighted astonishment. Oliver, feeling the occasion must be met, leant forward with a truly radiant expression, and said:

"By Jove, Breeze, do you really mean it?"

"Of course I mean it," replied Breeze, flicking his cigar-ash nonchalantly into a tray. "I flatter myself that novelists of our young friend's calibre never wait long before they find themselves in the *Cecil*. I suppose you've still got your ridiculous notion that because we reach a large public we cannot print the best! That's where you make the biggest mistake of your life!"

"No, no, no, you misunderstand me," said Oliver rapidly, as he flashed an impatient frown at the silent

Thurlow. "I knew you got the best, but I confess I thought you waited until they were more widely known than Edmund is."

"It has always been our boast," remarked Mr. Breeze, "that we are always first in the field. Now, come, come, Mr. Thurlow, what can you send me? Have you got a finished story by you?"

"Well, yes, I have," replied the genius, "but I don't suppose you'll like it."

"And why?" enquired Breeze.

"Oh, I don't know . . ."

"I rather doubt," resumed the Editor, "whether you have the faintest notion what I am likely to like or dislike. Tell me, now, has it an English background?"

"I'm afraid," said Thurlow, "it's about two Polish people in Warsaw."

"Good Lord," said Breeze, "that won't do. Paris is all right, Russia's all right, Italy sometimes; but not all those countries out there. Wouldn't it be possible to change it to England?"

"Oh, easily. It was only that I imagined it when I was in Warsaw. It's just a matter of altering names."

"Good. Send that story along and I'll print it—star it, too!" An afterthought occurred to him. "But it isn't," he asked, "blasphemous, I presume?"

"No," replied Thurlow, trying to prevent his face from looking too rigid.

"Or obscene?"

"I'm never quite sure what that word means . . . but no, no."

"Or political?"

"Certainly not."

"Then I'll take it, on the spot. Whatever it's like, your name will carry it. The artist is entitled to express himself in his own way, I have always said; and the best have always had an open platform in the *Cecil*."

Oliver interrupted again.

"It's hardly my affair, of course, Breeze, but we both know—no, you mustn't mind, Edmund—how unpractical these imaginative writers often are. You've mentioned nothing about a price."

"Don't bother about that," said Thurlow, with a touch of impatience, "we can leave that to Mr. Breeze."

"I'm sorry, Edmund," insisted Oliver, "but I don't think it would be right. You see, Breeze, Edmund could get a very large price indeed from one of the magazines which do things on a bigger scale than yours."

Breeze was in a rage, suddenly. He tried to say, "Well, damn your eyes, let him!" but he simply couldn't. No, he'd got to show this reptile, who had been pretending to be so agreeable. His tone, when his voice at last emerged from strangulation, had a rasp in it: "I should be glad to be informed which these magazines are."

Oliver smoothed him down. "Please don't mistake my meaning, Breeze; the most lavish papers are not necessarily the soundest. But I did hear the other day that the *Green* had paid Mr. Kipling . . ." and he whispered, with the air of keeping the figure diplomatically from Thurlow's ears.

This fantastic impudence took Mr. Breeze's breath away. Kipling . . . and Thurlow! But Walter Breeze was not going to be beaten.

"Very well, then," he said, in his best superman manner, "the *Cecil* will pay Mr. Thurlow precisely what the *Green* paid Mr. Kipling." He repeated the figure. "Does that satisfy you, Mr. Thurlow?" he asked.

Thurlow belonged to a generation not easily thrilled.

"Thanks very much," he replied; "it seems just about right."

But when Breeze had gone, his pent-up feelings broke out. Never, never again would he sit through lunch with such a creature. He'd keep his word this time and see the thing through, but he'd quite enough Breezes to last his lifetime.

"I do wish you weren't so highly strung," said Oliver, taking his arm: "but there, I suppose that if you weren't, there wouldn't be the quality that there is in your writing. Now remember what you said about being amenable to editorial suggestions, won't you?"

"I've promised, haven't I?"

"Well, promise again."

"I'll make any alterations the damned swine cares to suggest. There! Will that do?"

"Yes; that's better. And now let's go and see that Russian film."

III

It must not be supposed that Mr. Breeze himself read every manuscript which arrived at the office of the *Cecil*. Naturally, since the world is full of optimists who bombard editors of "fiction-magazines" with articles on Foreign Affairs, serials about Socialism, Odes to Pan, and contemplative essays by blind or bedridden aunts, the time of important persons can be saved by weeding-out, conducted by persons less important. But Mr. Breeze was relieved of far more than the obvious absurdities: for some years he had, in fact, though he never allowed himself to think it, been relieved of almost everything. For in Miss Firkins, his secretary, he had, as he frequently and heartily remarked to his friends and clients, "a treasure." The implication always was—and it was perhaps the desire of conveying that implication that moved him to celebrate her worth so often and so effusively—that she was especially good, in some mysterious way, at relieving an overburdened Titan of some mysterious pressure, as well as (of course) at shorthand, typewriting and the nice conduct of a cloudy telephone. Her office, though, had gradually come to cover a far greater field than that. Several years before, he had, one month, owing to the late withdrawal of a story which he discovered had already been printed in the pages of a rival, to fill up an unexpected gap in the forthcoming number. There was, annoyingly, nothing on hand of suitable length which could be put in without destroying the regular, careful balance between the thrilling, the sweet and the funny, and he cursed, in front of Miss Firkins, with unusually natural vigour. She stood there, slender, dark, very neat, self-contained, until the explosion was over, and then, with a shyness which he did not observe to be assumed, "ventured a suggestion." She had glanced, she said, one recent morning, over the manuscripts that she had reserved for him, and had noticed one which she thought would be ideally suitable. For a moment he was dominated by resentment that a chit of a girl should dare to have an opinion on such a subject; but time pressed, and he offhandedly told her to dig the story out of the drawer, and dismissed her.

"I think," she said as she went, "it will be very popular indeed."

"That's where you're wrong," he muttered to himself several times as he perused the manuscript. But it certainly passed muster, and in it went. Rather to his annoyance, its success exceeded any expectations that even Miss Firkins could have expected. Salesmanager, travellers, advertising men, they were all delighted. Stories reached him of bookstall clerks who had humorously complained that a few more such splendid stories as that would lead to their being dismissed for negligence of duty. "Stroke of luck," thought Mr. Breeze to himself, sneering at what he thought was a new smile of self-satisfaction on the face of Miss Firkins. All the same, it was not long before, feeling unequal to face a huge pile of waiting manuscripts and being in urgent need of something really good in the melodramatic way, he asked her to give the drawer a run through, adding, with jocular scepticism, "See if you can pull it off a second time." That was precisely what she did, and by gradual stages the present position had been reached. Miss Firkins read all the manuscripts and singled out those she thought would do; the rest were formally passed on for his opinion; but latterly he had not even pretended to glance at them, passing them over to her in stacks with "Shoot these back, Miss Firkins, will you?"

And there was no doubt of it, her judgment was consistently good. It annoyed him a little that a secretary, with no experience of Fleet Street whatever, and a mere woman to boot, should have a talent in this one direction which even his own did not surpass. "What they call a *flair*, I suppose," was his final summary of the position. It also irritated him that, whilst evidently knowing exactly what thousands of readers would like, Miss Firkins never betrayed the slightest personal interest in the stories she so highly recommended for publication. Once or twice in unguarded moments she had said things that suggested that she regarded stories and readers alike as being, in some extraordinary way, beneath her. Once, indeed, the word "tripe" had slipped from her lips when she was in the very act of passing on one of the most successful, and consequently one of the finest, stories they had had for years; the word would have been unseemly on the lips of any woman, much less on those of one who had pretensions to being a lady; and it was unpardonably rude and conceited of her to apply it to work by her betters. But he had checked his impulse to rebuke her: there at least he knew where he stood: he wasn't going to lose Miss Firkins if he could help it: she was much too valuable.

This morning the usual pile of envelopes was on the desk, with the usual annotations inscribed on them the previous afternoon. There was also one, adorned only with "Came this morning. Private Letter. Apparently Commissioned." He pressed the button of the office bell, and Miss Firkins appeared.

"Come here, Miss Firkins," he said. "Did you happen to glance at this story this morning?"

"Do you mean Mr. Thurlow's?"

"You've heard of him, then?"

"Why, of course; everybody reads him."

"Humph! Depends on what you mean by 'everybody.' But what do you think of the story?"

"If you mean me personally, I think it's extraordinarily interesting and beautifully written. But I don't think it would do in the *Cecil*."

"And why not?"

"Well, it's too . . ." she checked the word "intelligent" . . . "it's not at all our kind of story."

"I've told you before, I'll print anything that's good. Can't you put your objection any clearer?"

"Well . . . oh, well . . . I really think, Mr. Breeze, you'd better read it yourself and see what you think of it. Anyhow, you seem to have promised to print it."

"Under conditions I have. Very good."

She went.

Mr. Breeze read the story. Warsaw had disappeared and the leading characters were now called William and Jane, and lived in London. The farther he read the more bewildered he looked, and at moments anger apparently took the place of bewilderment. "Damned if I can understand half of it!" he exclaimed once; and then: "Lord, so this is what those highbrows like,

K

is it? Is this what they call beautiful?" Finishing it, he laid it down and relapsed into profound thought. His brain was working, not a doubt of it. Before long he came to a decision, and rang again for his secretary.

"Miss Firkins," he said, "there's a 'phone number on this notepaper of Mr. Thurlow's. See if you can get through to him."

She retired and within two minutes his bell trilled.

"Is that Mr. Thurlow?" he asked: then quick-fired a sequence of remarks, barely giving his interlocutor time to reply: "Just wanted to tell you, first-class story, first-class. . . . Yes, proud to print it. . . . Just one or two things, one or two small things. . . . Wouldn't take you five minutes. . . . Easier if you came and talked about it. . . . What about this afternoon? . . . All right, three o'clock, do excellently. . . . Looking forward to seeing you."

He put down the instrument, wiped his forehead, resumed the study of the manuscript and began to make notes on a pad.

IV

Mr. Breeze did not return after lunch until twenty minutes past three. Not that he minded that: it did authors no harm to be kept waiting a little—taught them they were not the only people in the world. He wore, however, an air of bustle when Miss Firkins responded to his summons.

"Hasn't Mr. Thurlow come?" he asked.

"Yes, he's been here since three."

"Where is he then?"

"Oh, he's been sitting in my room, talking to me."

Breeze frowned. "Bring him in at once."

She did. Thurlow was waved into an armchair by the desk, and provided with a Turkish cigarette, and the conversation began.

Breeze, he flattered himself, was a diplomatist, and knew human nature. "If you want a man to do a thing, make him think he wants to do it himself," was his motto; and he prided himself on his ability to lubricate the wheels of persuasion. His opening was tentative. He summarised the story as moderately as he could, threw out one or two casual suggestions by the way, noticed that they evoked no response from the so far obdurate author, and proceeded very delicately to hint at one or two improvements—just one or two to start with.

"I suppose you'll agree with me, Mr. Thurlow," he began, "that the essentials of a story are what matter, and that the subordinate details are of much less importance."

"Yes," said Thurlow.

"Let me mention a case in point," he went on, "just to show what I mean. The renunciation in your story takes place because the girl finds she has a hereditary disease, doesn't it?"

"Yes," replied Thurlow, with truth.

"Well, it's the renunciation that matters and leads to the rest, isn't it? and what the cause of it is is of no importance, provided it is adequate."

"I suppose not," said Thurlow, with that curious stare of his.

"For instance, she might be moved to precisely the same course of action if she were the only daughter of a mother who developed an incurable disease, and knew it to be her duty to live henceforth for her mother?"

"Yes, I suppose."

"Quite. Now I'm not suggesting this very trifling change without good and sufficient reason. Now ours, Mr. Thurlow, is—though by no means entirely, of course, far from it—in some measure a family paper."

Thurlow's wince was barely perceptible.

"And people—you can trust me to know—would think this notion of a heroine with a hereditary disease—well, as it were, unpleasant."

"I don't see anything wrong with a hereditary disease," replied Thurlow, "there are scores of them."

"I'm afraid you must take it from me. You're a great writer. But I have my job, too, and I know it from A to Z. Now will you, not to please me, but for your own sake, modify your story to this extent?"

Thurlow paused. But, after all, he was pledged to go through with it.

"Yes, Mr. Breeze, I'll do that," he said.

Breeze rubbed his hands. "Splendid, splendid!" he observed encouragingly. "So far so good. Now, by the same token, since it is the renunciation of the young lovers that matters, the story will be just as significant whoever they are."

"Yes. I told you it was an accident. I originally made them Poles."

"I didn't mean that; I'm not thinking of nationality now, but of social position. Now we're both perfectly aware that, theoretically, city clerks and milliners have precisely the same feelings as the rest of us. But you can't call them *romantic*, you know; they don't even think so themselves. Plenty of poor people read the *Cecil*, and I can assure you—I *know*—that they'd like your story ten thousand times better if it let them into the feelings of somebody who was *above* themselves."

At this point, for the first time, a faint smile played about Thurlow's mouth; the tension of his resistance was over, and, in a flash, he decided not merely that he must go all the way, but that the farther he went the more preposterously ironical the situation would be. In that one second he became a better novelist with a wider scope.

"Would it do," he said, in the voice of a humble

novice speaking to a senior master of his craft, "if he was a baronet?"

Mr. Breeze paused and thought.

"Yes," he replied, "I should think that would be the best thing of all for a story of your type. You are, after all, a realist, and a peerage mightn't sound quite so convincing."

Thurlow leaned forward, young, grim, pale, intent.

"No," he agreed emphatically, "you are absolutely right. Peers have something more remote and fantastic about them, haven't they? You shall have the story amended within a week, Mr. Breeze. Will that do?"

"Admirably, my dear fellow, admirably," said Breeze, rising in a manner which suggested an end to the interview. "There's only just one thing," he added, as he shook hands.

"Yes?"

"I may think of just one or two more suggestions after you've gone. Quite small, quite small. You've been very reasonable; much more than most of these young fellows: I shall watch your career with interest. You won't mind if I drop you a note to-night, will you?"

"Most certainly not," replied the young man. "I shall be glad to benefit by any suggestion you may care to make."

"Good-bye, then, good-bye."

Thurlow went out. It seemed to Mr. Breeze that

there was a sound as of a door closing, as it might have been Miss Firkins'; but perhaps that was only imagination. When, a quarter of an hour afterwards, he rang for Miss Firkins, he rather thought he heard a murmur of voices and then steps going down the stairs. But why give way to uneasy conjectures?

The trim secretary came in, and waited inquiringly.

"Get this letter to Mr. Thurlow off at once, please. I want it to reach him to-night." He did not think it necessary to explain that the letter contained the last small suggestion that the story should be given a Happy Ending. After all, the doctors might easily have diagnosed the mother's disease wrongly, and the Love of the Lovers would have been tested just as thoroughly if all quite suddenly came right just at the end.

Miss Firkins paused at the door. "Oh, Mr. Breeze," she remarked, in a matter-of-fact way, "shall I get his cheque for Mr. Thurlow? He told me as he was going out that you'd promised him payment as soon as you'd definitely accepted the story."

Breeze flushed and bridled. "Why couldn't he have asked for it himself," he said harshly, "instead of sneaking round to my secretary?"

Miss Firkins was not at a loss. "I think he saw that himself," she replied, "but the poor boy was too shy."

"All right," mumbled the Editor, "bring me

the cheque and I'll sign it."

V

There were several more visits, letters and revisions before, after a month, Thurlow was sent a proof for final correction. It came back from him by an afternoon post: Miss Firkins brought it in in her hand.

Breeze half turned his head. "So it's ready for press now?" he asked.

"Yes, Mr. Breeze."

"Send it through, then."

"There are one or two small alterations that I think you ought to pass your eye over."

"All right, give it here." He laid it on the desk before him.

"And, Mr. Breeze . . ."

"Well?"

"I'm frightfully sorry. I'm sure you'll easily find somebody better. But I should like to go at the end of the month."

Breeze leapt up as though shot. "Wha-a-t?" he gasped.

"Please don't be upset. But it simply *can't* be helped. You see, I'm going to be married."

He sat down again, torn between rage and utter dejection.

"Whom are you marrying?"

"Mr. Thurlow!"

The editor's eyes bulged; he gripped the arms of his chair. "Good Lord in Heaven," he whispered, "it can't be! What, that little . . . !" and checked himself. "How long has this been going on, may I ask?"

Miss Firkins remained perfectly cool. "Oh, we made friends, you see, that first day, when he came here and had to wait for you."

His gaze wandered into infinity. He did not notice her as she quietly slipped out of the room. The bottom of his universe had fallen out, and all because he had generously patronised one of those beastly highbrows! Rage and misery still contested the field. At last, with a titanic effort, he brought himself back to the immediate. He picked up Thurlow's final proof.

The alterations were inconsiderable. The story was in the last agreed form. But the names of hero and heroine throughout had been altered (with the marginal note, "Do you mind? If you do, leave them as they were. E.T.") into Sir Edwin and Lady Angelina.

PROFESSOR GUBBITT'S REVOLUTION

PROFESSOR GUBBITT'S REVOLUTION

I

THROUGHOUT the year 1929 a good deal of attention was devoted by *The Times* newspaper to certain excavations conducted at St. Albans by Dr. R. E. Mortimer Wheeler and the usual concomitant of "a devoted staff of male and female assistants." Dr. Wheeler was excavating the site of the Roman City of Verulamium, and great interest was aroused by the gradual unveiling of house and temple and forum. In the same year rather less attention was devoted in the advertisement and "Real Estate" columns of the same great newspaper to the fact that Gorhambury, the ancestral seat of Lord Verulam and once the home of Francis Bacon, was in the market. But no attention whatever was paid to an excavation at Gorhambury, far more exacting than Dr. Wheeler's, for the simple reason that no one heard anything about it.

No one knew that the cheerful plump gentleman with a brown beard who arrived at Gorhambury with an "Order to View" the extensive domain, and a fine assumption of interest in bathrooms and pheasant-covers, was Professor Skinner J. Gubbitt, of Jones

University, Rhode Island, for the simple reason that the Professor when presenting himself, had given a false name—a name, indeed, familiar wherever pork and beans are consumed, in other words, everywhere. Only the retainers who took him over the estate knew that he appeared especially interested in a certain corner of the park, in which the extremely old, gnarled and cavernous trunk of an oak tree was conspicuous, and then oddly asked to be led straight to the nearest point in the park wall, which reached, he looked over and seemed very interested in the features of the road outside. And only his wife, who was also his chauffeur, knew that late that night, when the moon shone frostily on a cold and solitary park, he was driven to that point, scaled the wall carrying a pick-axe and shovel, and, half-an-hour later, scaled it again, after handing over to his wife the pick-axe and shovel and a small metal box. Next day nobody noticed, for nobody came near the spot, that somebody had been digging at the foot of the blasted oak. And, whoever may have known, few much cared that a cheerful little bearded professor and his wife, feeling inclined to celebrate a great occasion, had cancelled their passage in the small and crowded *Carbolic* and engaged the largest and most expensive Louis Quinze suite on the *Kleptomania*, which they just managed to catch that evening. . . .

At Verulamium, they went on digging for the

foundations of Roman bakers' shops.

Sir Sidney Lee's *Life of Shakespeare* continued to be studied in the Universities.

The town of Stratford reposed happily on the profits of last summer's trade.

And, night after night, in the upper chamber of a comfortable frame-house in Grant Avenue, Jonestown, Professor Skinner J. Gubbitt, fortified by synthetic gin and orange juice, worked steadily at a small book and, having finished his book, at a series of long and (he flattered himself) sensational newspaper articles.

II

On 3rd April, 1930, the London newspapers all contained news from New York, the more popular press making much more of it than the organs of weight and standing. The following, with much else, was spread across the front page of the *London Daily Sun*:

BACON!!
Shakespeare Authorship Proved
U.S. Professor's Lead Box
and New York Believes It!
(From our New York Correspondent, *B. S. Finkelstein*)

This morning the whole of the front page of the *New*

York Moon is devoted to the Final Proof that Bacon wrote Shakespeare—even the massacre of fifty-three Chicago gangsters by means of flammenwerfers is relegated to a back page. The discoverer is Professor Skinner J. Gubbitt, of Jones University.

The Professor, with a wealth of detail, describes how he found cipher clues in the plays pointing to the foot of a certain tree at Gorhambury Park (where Bacon died) as the cache of a leaden box containing Bacon's own confession, and a number of other papers including an unpublished play, *Alexander the Great*, alleged to be in Bacon's handwriting and the finest thing "Shakespeare" ever wrote. A page of this is printed in facsimile.

Several more instalments are promised, including "Revelations" about the character of what the newspaper calls "The Stratford Impostor."

The story is certainly fully annotated. Before publication the *Sun* obtained the opinions of two hundred and forty Presidents of Universities, Mr. John D. Rockefeller, senr., Senator Blaine, and the Mayor of New York. They all, in short messages, explain that they were incredulous at first, but then absolutely convinced.

The early evening papers all proclaim the dethronement of Shakespeare, except the *Meteor*, which asks why 1st April was not chosen, says that the extract from the "new" plays reads like Edgar Guest, and prints a series of "interviews" with Al Capone, Mrs. Aimee Macpherson, Harold Bell Wright, Greta Garbo, and Mickey the Mouse, who all announce their intention of standing by Shakespeare.

All the same, New York is convinced.

The *Sun*, though ridiculing the whole story in its editorial columns, announces that "in view of the importance of the issue involved," it had arranged with the Professor and the New York newspaper, to have the whole story cabled day by day by photo-telegraphy.

Meanwhile it published short interviews with Sir Oliver Lodge and Sir Arthur Keith, who expressed contempt for so stupid a fraud, and messages as follows:

"Sure there must be some terrible mistake some-where."—*Mr. John Galsworthy.*

"Our King shall never be discrowned."—*Mr. John Masefield.*

"What does it matter who wrote such romantic and reactionary rubbish?"—*Mr. G. Bernard Shaw.*

"If they insist on Bacon we shall give them Beans." —*Mr. G. K. Chesterton.*

And, flaming across the leader-page, written with that white heat of ardour, that wealth of metaphor and repetition, and that marvellous speed, for which he is

L

justly famous, was a "Passionate Protest," by Mr. John Dumbbell, of which the following may serve as typical:

. . . A fig for this American professor. A fig for all professors. A fig? No! rather a fig-leaf to cover his shame!

He is a spoilator of literary shrines. He is a trampler in the Temple of the Muses. But his bomb-shell will prove a boomerang which will batter his own poor vain-glorious skull. It will hammer him on the head. It will pound him upon the pate. . . .

No, he shall not rob us of our Shakespeare. Shakespeare is ours, of the flesh and bone and fibre of us. The Swan of Avon was never miraculously hatched to be the plaything of professors or the prey of pedants. He is as English as the English sun, he is as English as the English rain. He is as Celtic as the mist and as Saxon as the soil. Our Shakespeare knew well enough how to lash pompous professors. Our Shakespeare could have scourged this schoolmaster. Our Shakespeare could have withered and wilted with the great Warwickshire gusts of his laughter this Yankee Holofernes, this Jabberer from Jonesville, this pestiferous purveyor of Bacon! Bacon, forsooth! Bacon, that cold-faced lawyer! Bacon, that sly and prudent essayist! Bacon, that immoral moralist! Bacon, that Mr. Worldly Wiseman! Bacon, that taker of bribes!

Bacon, that worshipper of Mammon! No, Bacon was not Shakespeare. If he was anybody he was Shylock.

I tell this American professor, I tell all the Americans and all the professors, that though they may take the shirt off our backs they shall not take our Shakespeare. He is the glory of our manhood. He is the pride of our womanhood. He is the brightest star in Britain's crown. He is as English as the bluebells in the English brakes. . . .

This, though not everybody would have put it in the same way, was the general opinion of all Great Britain on the morning of 3rd April.

III

But the tune changed the next morning; and when the editors who had printed only short paragraphs on the "canard," and the jesters who had written frolicsome leaderettes, saw their *Sun*, on the 4th, they began to have doubts. There were some consolations for them. There were swarms more "messages" expressing contempt. The Prime Minister of Queensland had announced that Australians would stand by Shakespeare, and even from across the Atlantic there were certain grains of consolation. Numbers of novelists had declared the page from *Alexander* to be rubbish, and the State Congress of Tennessee, in special session at Dayton, had resolved unanimously that any teacher in the State Schools who referred to the name of Bacon in the schools should be summarily dismissed. That was all very well; and of course the vast mass of the population of England which takes any interest in Shakespeare, but is unequipped for the scrutiny of documentary or æsthetic evidence, was either indignant or hilarious at what must obviously be a gigantic hoax. Unfortunately the minority capable of such scrutiny did not take long to come to the conclusion that there was a very strong case to be answered.

To start with, there was the reputation of Gubbitt. He may have gone mad of course, or have become suddenly greedy for glory at whatever expense of unscrupulousness. But he had, in the small world of Elizabethan scholarship, a reputation for learning and accuracy, and, once, for a day, he had been celebrated all over the world because of a triumph of research. Working in the inexhaustible mine of the Public Record Office, he had discovered a document which added one more to the short list of "genuine Shakespeare signatures." As usual the document had something to do with money and law. The greatest of poets was apparently engaged in foreclosing a mortgage on a small cheesemonger. But there it was, as everybody said, a Momentous Addition to the slender structure of Shakespearean Biography: "Step by step," scores of eminent writers had said, "we are gradually accumulating materials which are revealing to us what manner of being this Shakespeare was, the very man who lived, and walked and talked in the animated and many-coloured England of Elizabeth's day." Gubbitt's reputation, in fact, was among the highest of its time.

That only went so far. But if his first set of documents were fakes, what marvellous fakes they were! His account of the steps by which he was led to Baconianism and the oak at Gorhambury was not impressive: though that was perhaps because (as he frankly stated) he had no space for his vast train of clues in a newspaper, and for the full history of his search the public would have to wait for his book—of which, it was stated, half a million copies had been already subscribed in advance, in two days. He only very sketchily referred to a variety of passages, which made a connected story. There were several from the grave-digging scene in *Hamlet*, including the snatch, "A pick-axe, and a spade, a spade": the professor even casually remarked that there came a point when the fabric of hidden narrative was so clear that he felt quite sure what buried play he would find from the passage:

Ham.—Dost thou think Alexander looked o' this fashion i' the earth?

HOR.—E'en so.

A long and painful pursuit of key-sentences from play to play had led him to the Leaden Casket in *The Merchant of Venice* and another to the oak around which was played the masquerade in *The Merry Wives*. Very many of the ciphers unveiled by previous Baconians had been of assistance to him, but it was by a route new to all of them that he had reached the clinching finale of the familiar "Hic hæc hog"—"Hear that Bacon." Ingenious though it all was, it might well have been picked to pieces had the learned detective merely predicted the finding of the box. But he said he had found it.

There, in handwriting which no expert could distinguish from Bacon's acknowledged script, were extracts of a confession telling the whole story of his concealment in the interests of his career, of his employment of the theatrical manager, of his preparation of a hiding-place the search for which—and he admitted his diabolical amusement at the thought— would rack the brains of generations, and of his abandonment of the muse shortly after Shakespeare's very inconvenient death. There were receipts, signed in Shakespeare's cramped scrawl, for moneys paid, which explained the age-long mystery of his wealth and the coat-of-arms and the fine house at Stratford. His much-discussed indolence at the end of his life was explained by Bacon being too busy to write plays. All these papers might have been questioned, though only by those who will question anything. But the extract from *Alexander* commanded instant recognition by all the greatest poets and critics in England.

It is unnecessary to quote at this date that glorious speech, the most musical, the most passionate, the richest in imagery of all Shakespeare's speeches, in which Alexander addresses his mistress. It is now familiar to the lips of every child in England, and I cannot bring myself to waste space upon it. But it clinched matters.

IV

Within two days the principal cartoonist of *Punch* was engaged on a cartoon of an ironic Bacon holding out for inspection a copy of the 1623 edition of the plays, the inscription underneath being, "The First Foolio." *The Times* announced its final conversion in a leading article two columns long. It began:

After some hesitation we have come to the conclusion that the irrefutability of Professor Skinner Gubbitt's proofs that the works of Shakespeare were actually written by the most illustrious of all Lord Chancellors can no longer be resisted. The consequences of this revolution are sufficient to strike awe into all who pause to contemplate them. He who has so often been termed, "The Wisest of Mankind," must henceforth be also recognised as "The Noblest of Mankind"; and we must endeavour, as best we may, to reconcile our incredulous minds to the almost incredible truth that from the lips which expressed such profound truths and such a world of learning and speculation in "that other harmony" of prose, fell also the most majestic and the loveliest music which ever proceeded from mortal man. The hand which wrote the *Novum Organum* wrote also the woodland felicities of *As You Like It*, and the sober brain which might have been thought to have put forth its fullest powers in *The Advancement of Learning* was capable also of the tragic abandonment of Lear, and deigned to confess its kinship with the humble generality of mankind in the persiflage of a Beatrice and the lusty buffoonery of a Falstaff.

Yet, when we pause to think, the larger incredibility seems to lie elsewhere: to repose in the strange fact that for centuries we should all have found it possible to accept as a conceivable author of "Shakespeare's Works" such a personage as is, imperfectly, but all too adequately, revealed in the standard "lives" of the ci-devant Swan of Avon. The son of a petty tradesman in a provincial town,

etc. Educated (if educated at all) at, etc. . . .
Thrown at an early age, etc. . . . Known beyond
dispute, to have been a secondary theatrical manager
by profession, with a grasping and mercenary
speculation in houses and land as subsidiary (if it
was subsidiary) employment, he was surely the least
suitable of all candidates for such a throne as that on
which his ghost has now for three centuries mas-
queraded. Illusions similar in kind, it may be, have
prevailed as long, but none surely, etc. . . .

It must be obvious that an ample and unqualified
reparation is now due to the memories of the late
Mrs. Gallup, the late Mr. Pott, the late Sir Edwin
Durning Lawrence, the late Colonel Snook, and
others of that gallant band of pioneers, who, in face
of every species of discouragement, held aloft long
since those torches of truth by whose light Professor Gubbitt has at last penetrated into the inmost
recesses of the secular secret. Imperfectly provided,
perhaps, as some of them, etc. . . .

As for Professor Gubbitt, it is plain that for all
time the whole English-speaking world, nay, the
whole of mankind, will lie sempiternally in his debt.
Not only, etc. . . . Not only, etc. . . . But, by
restoring the first of all the crowns of poetry to its
rightful head, he has resolved an age-long dis-
cordance and provided us at last with a "Shakespeare" whose known intellectual splendour and

dignity of person and station conform to what all the world has always felt must have been the inevitable attributes of the creator of a Hamlet and the friend of a Southampton, etc. . . .

On the following day, in his most popular newspaper, Mr. John Dumbbell made the handsomest and most rapid recantation which even his hand had ever penned. His article on the first day had been headed, "They Shall not Steal our Shakespeare!" The nature of this one, as vehement, as bravely unqualified, as richly festooned with stock metaphors and redundancies, was headed, "The Glory that was Bacon!" Its tenor may briefly be illustrated:

. . . The last rags of pretence have been stripped from the Great Impostor. His head is bowed. The last of his stolen pence have dropped from his hand. His back is bared to the lash. He is fixed for ever in a posthumous pillory. He is seated for ever in the stocks of the unquenchable laughter of mankind.

Shakespeare the Stratford lout! The son of a peddling pork merchant! The son of a bankrupt! The tenth-rate actor who married because marry he must! The rapacious usurer whose every signature attests his miserliness and ruthlessness! The snob who must buy him a coat-of-arms! The smug Philistine who must lord it at Stratford over his betters! The meanly and crawling creature who carried his petty revenges beyond the grave, bequeathing to his wife his second-best bed! He was as illiterate as a Hottentot. He was as dense as a London fog. He was as obtuse as the obtusest of angles. He stands in his nakedness now as what he was, smearing his avarice even across the fairest pages of poesy. A pimp of literature. A pandarus of drama. A greedy go-between of the Arts. . . . A. . . .

But Bacon! He, the broad-browed Verulam, is "now for ever England." Bacon is a part of England. Bacon *is* England. Bacon is as English as the English sun. He is as English as the English rain, as the violets of Verulamium and the bluebells in his Hertfordshire woods. Eternal fame will belaurel his brow. Everlasting brightness will clothe his forehead. He is the Swan of St. Albans. He is the Giant of Gorhambury.

But, as Bacon would have said, "enough of that, Hal, an thou lovest me."

v

The vast reverberations all over the world of the discovery cannot fully be recounted here. It must suffice to quote a few from the millions of short paragraphs which for months, in numbers which first multiplied and then dwindled, covered the pages of the world's newspapers. I give them without dates or sources:

At yesterday's meeting of the Dover Town Council it was unanimously resolved that Shakespeare's Cliff should henceforward be known as Bacon's Cliff.

The Shakespeare Memorial Theatre at Stratford will, it is announced, be reopened next week as the Palace Picturedrome.

Interviewed yesterday, Signor Mussolini said that he did not care two lire whether Bacon or Shakespeare wrote the plays. It was a pity, said His Excellency, that foreigners should write plays about Italy without any knowledge of the country. Such a booby as Antonio, added Il Duce, could not be found throughout the length and breadth of Italy. Il Capo di Governo concluded by saying that Fascism had come and would stay.

Last night the statue of Shakespeare in Leicester Square was painted green, it is believed by hospital students. To-day the Westminster City Council decided that it might as well be left in that condition pending its replacement by a statue of Lord Bacon.

The Bacon National Theatre committee have

issued an appeal to the Press and public not to refer to the great dramatist as Lord Bacon. This is a solecism. His proper style was Francis Bacon, Lord Verulam.

In the House of Commons this afternoon loud and general laughter was evoked by a slip on the part of the Leader of the Opposition. He inadvertently alluded to the author of *Othello* as "Shakespeare." "Bacon," "Bacon" came from all sides. "Too late to save it, I fear," dryly remarked Mr. Baldwin: at which there was a renewed burst of general laughter, in which the right honourable gentleman heartily joined.

The Bolivian Parliament has voted three million pesetas for the erection of a statue to Bacon in the principal square of El Paz.

Yesterday, at the annual Curers' Conference at Trowbridge, Wilts., the Chairman, Mr. A. March-Hare, raised a novel point. All his life, he said, he had been a devotee of the works of our National Bard, and now he could not help feeling guilty of something like blasphemy every morning when he went down to the works, and saw "Bacon Factory" displayed across the façade. Mr. Brown (Salisbury) said that he agreed that the prevention of Bacon being now no longer possible it was hardly seemly to attempt his cure. Mr. Higgs (Devizes) agreed, stating that it would be very ambiguous in future to use such phrases as "steeped in the study of Bacon," "giving the children a true insight into Bacon." Mr. Nitwit (Yorkshire Ham Growers, York) said that it would be a proper punishment for the Pirate of Stratford, who had rewarded his helpless bene- factor by publishing illicit quartos of the plays, were his name to be substituted for Bacon's where their commodity was concerned. Let them, in future, refer to "a side of Shakespeare," "a rasher of Shakespeare," "Shakespeare and Eggs," and "Liver and Shakespeare." It would serve Shakespeare right. Ultimately it was agreed to ask the British Academy and the Editors of the Oxford Dictionary to suggest a new name which should be attractive, preferably one not connected with literature. A Scottish member's amendment that, in the interests of the memory of the Ettrick Shepherd, the source of bacon should no longer be termed "Hog" was ruled out of order as irrelevant.

Parliament has been asked for a special grant to enable the British Museum to re-catalogue the tens of thousands of entries in the "Shakespeare" volumes in the Library.

It is reported from Moscow that the Comintlit (C.I.L.) has decided that throughout the U.S.S.R., anyone mentioning the name of Professor Gubbitt or Bacon shall be shot as a person of counter- revolutionary mentality. The *Pravda* declares that the whole Gubbitt movement is a capitalist plot, whose object is to show that plays like Shakespeare's could only be written by an aristocrat. Shakespeare's father, adds the *Pravda*, was at worst a Kulak.

So it went: the vast boom in Bacon First Editions, including even his *Life of Henry VII*, the world-wide renaming of streets and squares, the rush on the stationers' shops for new notepaper for the countless Shakespeare societies, committees, theatres, taverns.

VI

There were repercussions everywhere. To the publishing trade, which had been going through a very bad time in the early months of 1930, the event was a godsend. For the rights in Professor Gubbitt's own book (which sold a million copies in Britain before the year ended) too great a sum was asked for any individual firm to produce. The Publishers' Association therefore formed an *ad hoc* company, in which all its members took shares, and was able, acting thus solidly, to make a bargain which was advantageous to the whole trade. Every book about "Shakespeare" which discussed his life or authorship was superseded, but the demand for new books covering the ground in a Baconian sense far more than compensated for this, whilst thousands of subjects for new books, on the newly-integrated corpus of Bacon's life and works, leapt at once to the eye of scholarship. Everybody was reading Bacon; even in the House of Commons the old habit of quotations was resumed; and in the universities, whose dons had always bitterly resisted the "Baconian Theory" with an utter inability to understand their own interests, hundreds of experts were flung into a new activity and a new prosperity. The West End theatres enjoyed such a season as they had never enjoyed since the golden days of musical comedy. Hitherto it had been a maxim in London that "Shakespeare did not pay." But at the height of the season of 1930, every single theatre in the West End was playing Bacon, and every single play of Bacon's could be seen in the West End, with the exception of *Pericles*—and that was running at the Old Vic. Stimulated by the flow of riches, the managers of London rose to impresarious heights which even they had never scaled before. There were three competing productions of *Othello*, in which the chief rôle was taken by a real Moor, a real Turk, and a real negro respectively. Troilus was acted by a real Greek, Florizel by a real Bohemian, Hamlet by a real Dane, Macbeth by a real Scotchman; and there was a tremendously ambitious performance of *The Merchant of Venice* in which all the parts were taken by real Italians, except those of Shylock and Jessica, which

were played by real Jews, and those of the foreign
suitors, which gave opportunities to a real Englishman, a real Frenchman and a real German. At
Hammersmith, Sir Nigel Playfair produced *Henry IV*
in Restoration Dress, with candelabra, songs, and
dances, himself leading the minutes as a periwigged
Falstaff: on the first night programme, by a happy turn
of wit, the Boar's Head, Eastcheap, appeared as the
Bacon's Head. Smart society had never been known to
talk so long about any one topic as it talked about the
sensation of the hour. These paragraphs, from the
Gossip column (22nd June, 1930) of Mr. Snooper, in
the *Daily Glimpse*, might be paralleled from any of its
issues over a period of months:

In St. James's Street I met Lord Mount Antler,
just back from his place at Glenvommit. His
fondness for Bacon's plays, of course, has always
been widely known. "I always knew," he observed,
"that those plays must have been written by a
gentleman. Of course, I have nothing against Shakespeare personally, but one *can* generally tell, I
find." General Fitzhugh, he said (no mean authority),
had always agreed with him. A moment later I ran
into Lady Badshot. She is the best-dressed woman
in England, but also, of course, the wittiest. She
told me that the boom in Bacon would certainly
mean the return of the pork-pie hat. Was she

M

serious? What do you think?

So, to lunch, at the quietest and selectest of French restaurants, not a hundred miles from Covent Garden. I rather agreed with Captain "Tuggles" Pearson, who says, of course, that he always goes there because there isn't a band. "How on earth," he always asks, "can a man be expected to eat and listen to a band at the same time? It stands to reason, doesn't it?" Yesterday he had with him a famous amateur jockey, who agreed with him. My equestrian friend had only one objection to the recent Transformation of the Bard. He had been asked to a Bacon dinner. "Dash it all," he very truly said, "a fellow cannot help what he feels, can he? And although I know it's all imagination, I cannot bring myself to face a Bacon dinner." He meant, of course, that it was the wrong time of day. However, the Curers' Congress resolution may ultimately get that put right.

At the next table were pretty Miss Peggy Pumpernickel, Lady "Vi" Gilderoy (just back from the Lido) and Princess "Baba" Attabetzkoy. "A hen-party, you see," said the Princess. "So were the three Graces," I could not help replying. They had all been to Gray's Inn, on a Bacon party; following the poet's footsteps through ancient courts and halls, and listening to the rooks in Bacon's Walk. "I think he must have written, 'Maud' as well," said Lady "Vi," with her quizzical smile. "It describes the rooks so beautifully."

So the world wagged. Parliament rose. The League of Nations assembly met. Il Duce made speeches. M. Briand made plans. Mr. Bradman made runs. The film stars made eyes. The theatres made money. The Conservative party made mistakes. Mr. Gandhi made trouble. The farmers made hay of their grass, the departments made hay of their business, Mr. Snowden made mincemeat of everybody; and Professor Gubbitt made two hemispheres talk incessantly of one subject, the climax being reached when he began his lecture-tour, which culminated with an address to the British Association, an official luncheon at the Guildhall, the presentation of the Freedom of the City of St. Albans, and the conferment of so many honorary degrees as to set at least one tottering firm of robe-makers on its feet. The British Association address was especially fascinating. Dr. Gubbitt showed, step by step, how Shakespeare, having Bacon in his grip, made a little extra money "on the side" by publishing those early quartos, whose imperfections have for so long bewildered the student; and with great cogency he managed to relate to each other the constant impecuniosity of Bacon with the perpetually increasing prosperity of the blood-sucking parasite at Stratford. The last outposts in the British Empire had fallen; it looked as though the battle was to all intents and purposes over, and the main effects of the change achieved. But as the summer wore on a cloud appeared on the horizon. Things were going very badly in Stratford, and it looked as though the whole of South Warwickshire would have to face a desperately hard winter.

VII

For amid all the frantic excitements and disputes, jests and junketings, conferences and celebrations of those spring and early summer months, a world beflagged with Bacon had overlooked one thing: the economic consequences of the change, as it affected certain portions of England. That St. Albans was going to benefit went without saying, and so, for some time, was hardly said: though there was a certain amount of talk when the prospectus of a Verulam Preservation and Development Company appeared in the papers, complete with Directors, Auditors, Brokers, Solicitors, Bankers, Promoters' consideration, and prospective dividends. That swarms of people were visiting St. Albans and Gorhambury was also observed, and also taken for granted; but the full implication of this, as augury of a permanent local industry, was hardly realised: there was so much else to talk about. Of Stratford, for some time, very little was heard. After all, Stratford was now "off the map."

Stratford, at the end of the first week, had had a little burst of notoriety. Its Town Council, especially convened, had debated the problem of authorship with all the fierce unanimity of a vested interest fighting for its life. When everybody else in England had been converted, Stratford remained passionately Shakespearean. One meeting, and one meeting only, of that municipal corporation, over which, so long ago, John Shakespeare (not yet insolvent) had presided, was reported in the London Press as fully as any session of Parliament. Then the curtain fell. A joke or two was made when it was learned that the Shakespeare Festival was still to be held. There were more humorous comments when the Chairman of the Brewery Company which owned the famous Hamlet Arms at Stratford announced to an Extraordinary General Meeting of Shareholders that their Board (as usual insuring as fully as possible against future risks) had some years since acquired the freehold of the Frozen Pullet at St. Albans, a house full of old oak, which he was sure, when it had been suitably equipped with copper warming-pans, would be uniquely attractive to American and other visitors. Otherwise Stratford, for the rest of the world, relapsed into the condition of the neighbouring Stow-on-the-Wold, the only worshippers left at the once venerated shrine being a few stray Fundamentalists from the more backward of the Southern States. Motorists whirled through its streets; few trains now stopped at its station.

Not until July was it that Mr. John Drinkwater, making his annual attempt to visit Mamble, first drew general attention to the acute distress now prevailing in Stratford. It was as though a great agricultural district had had, not a poor crop, but no crop at all, no single ear of wheat, not a root, not a fruit, not a blade of grass even. A whole town was out of work, and its ruin was spreading far and wide over the surrounding districts, half of whose capital had, directly or indirectly, been invested in the Shakespeare industry. Publicans were starving, lodging-house keepers were starving, not a postcard a week had been sold by the stationers, not a stick of chewing-gum by the confectioners, not a cigar by the tobacconists: a multitude of vergers, caretakers, and guides, who had spent years mastering the American language, now found the labour of years entirely wasted. Those who had always shown the industry and frugality of the ant were now faced, through no fault of their own, with a grasshopper's winter. Could not, Mr. Drinkwater inquired, a Mansion House Fund be opened for the distressed areas of South Warwickshire?

The Times, in an eloquent leader headed, "A Town upon the Dole," energetically supported the suggestion; and the Lord Mayor, Sir William Waterlow, was quick to respond. After all, there was the precedent of the Liberator Fund: there was, in essence, no difference between the innocent victims of Jabez Balfour's frauds and those of William Shakespeare's. Subscriptions poured in apace. Dr. Gubbitt, it is true, whose hatred of Stratford was of almost maniacal strength, refused to give a penny. But the big banking houses, the city companies, the newspaper peers, and a multitude of private persons rapidly brought the Fund to the respectable figure of £100,000; and especial note was taken of the generous behaviour of St. Albans, which had a local "Stratford Flag Day" in relief of the stricken inhabitants of the deposed birthplace. It seemed likely that the Fund would have to be turned into a permanent Trust for the benefit of the Stratford area when, in November, just as the worst of the cold weather was approaching, there happened a sudden event which rapidly replenished the tables of Stratford, and refuelled her fireplaces. Mr. G. K. Chesterton wrote an article which was like a thunderbolt. Seeing the obvious, as usual, long before anybody else, he transformed the situation at a stroke.

VIII

He wrote an essay in a very obscure weekly periodical. It was some days before anybody noticed it; but once it had met a human eye it spread like wildfire. His contention was simplicity itself:

It is a phenomenon (he wrote), very noticeable in human affairs, that if only a truth is large enough and simple enough it is almost certain to be overlooked. And through all these whirling months of Baconian festivity the most staggeringly simple of the major truths involved in Dr. Gubbitt's discovery has been ignored as most men habitually ignore the sky. As I write, the bugles of the world are sounding the Last Post over the grave of Stratford. But in a week or so, when one terrific platitude has at last been grasped, they will be sounding the Reveille. The Shakespeare Head, they say, lies in dust and ashes; it will rise from the ashes and shake the dust, if I may be pardoned the expression, from its feet. But in the innumerable Bore's Heads which have taken part in this discussion a tremendous truism will break with a violence like that of thunder and a radiance bright and irresistible as that of the dawn. . . .

For what is the one central fact about all this long debate? It is that the one old central fact which everybody used to know has now by everybody been forgotten. In the days before the days of the prophet Gubbitt one plain and powerful dogma was held in common by all those, of whom I was certainly one, who disputed, with vehemence, even with ferocity, Bacon's authorship of the plays then attributed to Shakespeare. We did not say that Shakespeare must have written the plays: for we knew very little about Shakespeare, and that little we did not like. What we said, and with constant and earnest repetition, was that nobody but a donkey or a don could conceivably think that the poetical works and the prose works were written by one and the same person. That was almost universally agreed. The ability to see that was the test of the ability to see anything. The capacity of denying that was the capacity of denying anything. The only truth that matters now is that that truth is still true. In other words, if, as we are now all convinced, Bacon wrote the plays, some other man must have written those voluminous prose works which we have always so greatly admired, but which, until recently, so few of us ever thought of reading.

Now, what follows must be as plain as a pikestaff to anybody who was not a member of the old and strict sect of Peculiar Primitive Baconians. We must find our man, and we are in as great a difficulty as ever we were before in finding a man who will answer our requirements unless that man is the man to whom we shall presently come. But our position now is infinitely stronger than it was then. Then we assumed that Shakespeare wrote the plays, because his name was on them, though we knew nothing whatever about him. But now we do know something about him, and that something is of crucial and indeed crushing importance. We know that Bacon employed him as an impersonator, that his duty, and his highly profitable duty, was to appear before his contemporaries as the creator of an imaginary world of men, the lyrist of *The Tempest*, the brooding dreamer from whom came like clouds the dark magnificence of Lear, the philosopher, and the scholar, whose eye had ranged over all history and whose vocabulary has been the despair of lexicographers. We are now asked to suppose that that stupendous responsibility was entrusted, and entrusted with staggering success, to a dolt and a lout who could probably neither read nor write. I have the greatest respect for my friend Mr. John Dumbbell; but no more preposterous theory was ever brought to the light outside the academies of Laputa. . . .

If a profound theologian wished somebody to father his works in public he would scarcely depute the work to a tub-thumping atheist from Hyde Park. If an eminent General wished somebody to make a speech for him at a public-school prize-giving he would hardly send as his substitute a rabid anti-militarist with a stutter and a strong Cockney accent. If I myself, I modestly suggest, desired to be impersonated successfully at a public dinner I should be rash (I am credibly informed) were I to entrust the onerous task to the Living Skeleton. The glaring deduction is that Shakespeare must have been a man who was, and could so appear to the world, roughly Bacon's equal in mind and manners. . . .

We shall not find a third, nor need we look for one. Bacon, we know, wrote the works of Shakespeare. The end of the proposition must (as Bacon said) "follow as the night the day." It is revealed in all its strange symmetrical beauty when we realise that nobody but Shakespeare can have written the works of Bacon.

And so it was. All the tensions were relieved and all the tragedies averted. Shakespeare, as *The Times* well said, might well rest content with the laurels of his achievement in "that other harmony of prose."

IX

All the tragedies save one. On the day which saw the simultaneous unveiling (by Mr. A. E. Housman) of the new statue of Bacon in Leicester Square, and (by Professor Einstein) of the new statue of Shakespeare outside the Imperial College of Science and

Technology, Dr. Gubbitt shot himself in the library of the great palace at Newport which he had so recently acquired from Mr. Vanderbilt. He left a note behind him. He was still, he said, a Baconian; he believed that Bacon wrote both those works which used to be attributed to Shakespeare and those which were now attributed to him. He felt convinced that patient study would discover in the prose works ciphered and other clues which would ultimately prove that the author of *Hamlet* was also the author of the *Essays*. Probably, somewhere at Gorhambury, there was another buried box. But he was tired and feeling old: and he could not face so Herculean a labour a second time.

THE ALIBI

THE ALIBI

"Stop it, Timmy," whispered Sir Richard, to the spaniel, who had whined.

The mere reflected the last pink flush of wintry sunset, and in the east, high above the far bed of rushes, the wisp of a moon was becoming distincter every time he looked at it. But it had rained in the afternoon when they had driven a few pheasants, and the black clouds massing on the northern horizon looked like more rain. It was getting cold. He blew on his fingers. Damn that fellow Henderson, for wanting to spin the day out like this, and his fluffy hysterical little wife for egging him on. Just because they had come to the duck-pond before—and she with them—chattering at the wrong moment too, just when the first big lot of duck came in. She probably had a pretty bad time with her husband. He remembered last year he had had suspicions of curses and sobbing. But women's admirations took strange directions. She obviously thought Henderson a Nimrod, and the brute was a rotten bad shot. Keen enough though, in all conscience: liked killing for its own sake, probably. Why do they saddle us with such M.P.'s—profiteers and Colonial adventurers, posing as Tories! Why on

earth had he let all the servants go to the fair: cold
supper! He was cold already. Again he stared from
the sodden little peninsula into the water. He leaned
his gun against the solitary tree and lit a cigarette, his
hands carefully shadowing the match and the glow of
the tip. And not even a man to look after the dog and
to carry the birds. Politeness to local members of
Parliament could go too far. Bad enough to have such
a bumptious blackguard to stay. And that foolish
little wife . . . back at the Manor . . . warm . . .
reading some silly novel, or confiding some nonsense
to that horrible set-faced companion of hers, with her
silent movements. How on earth could Henderson let
his wife saddle herself with such a death's head?

He heard a snipe but could not see it. He heard the
mew of plover, and a black stream of them flashed
across the fading sky and away into invisibility. Over
there, somewhere in those low thorns, Henderson was
crouching, and the width of the water between them.
The width of the water: the width of the world, he
thought. They had nothing in common at all. A
small foreboding gust of wind came over moor and
marsh, and rattled the leaves of the forlorn trees on the
high ridge behind him. It carried a sound with it, a
dim sort of brazen music, faint bangs and cries. It was
the fair. Three miles away! Doubtless the servants
were enjoying themselves. He closed his eyes and saw
the excited crowd in the lambent light of the flares,

roaring merry-go-rounds, cocoanut-shies, wheedling
gipsies with games of chance—or, rather, certainty!
He opened them, and there was the darkening solitude,
the damp wilderness that had been unchanged for
thousands of years. Naked savages had seen it so, and
on such dismal evenings thought the place bewitched.

He could hear nothing of the fair now. Silence was
only broken by the ghostly noises of the swamp,
twitters, rushes of wings, little flashes of fish, all eerie
now, causing the heart to tighten unreasonably,
ominous, as though some evil magnitude was brooding
over the place. Richard Moorhouse pulled down his
cape, drew the wet flaps of his collar together below
his damp beard, and shifted his position on the
squelching grass. Henderson was over there somewhere. Everybody knew the man was a swine, with
his red face and beastly curling moustache, his crooked
eyes and crooked companions. Except his wife of
course: perfectly obvious that nobody told her about
her precious husband's seraglio. Just the sort to go
mad out of jealousy: but she doted. Perhaps she was
more cunning than she looked: that companion, Mrs.
Rose, had eyes in her head; there was no saying what
women mightn't pour out to each other when they
were alone. He pulled himself together for the work
in hand, and passed his hand along the cold barrel of
his gun. The duck must surely come in now from
their mysterious haunts, if they were coming at all. If

N

they waited much longer the clouds would be up and across the struggling moon. The mirror of the water was growing darker. Plover cried again. How lonely it was! He stared hard across at Henderson's bank, but there was no form there now, merely a dark tract that was not water. There wasn't a sound anywhere. Henderson couldn't be there. He must have gone away and left him alone. Perhaps he was slinking away now! Weren't those footsteps again? How his nerves were on edge to-night! He would bet that Henderson had never noticed that car that seemed to stop near them just after they had got out, and would explain all those splashes as water rats. But that's what they probably were! A sound again! He whistled, a low wailing note, and waited. Across the water from that dim shore came a reply. Henderson was there, immobile, grim, ready. The whistle roused the dog again, whom he had forgotten. "Down you fool," he rasped, clouting the spaniel's head.

There was a faint unmistakable whirr of wings: he held his gun ready and peered at the dusk: there was a small splash and a faint contented quacking far to the right. It was almost too late. He'd give it five minutes more, then shout for Henderson, stretch his cramped limbs and stumble the half mile back to the car.

That faint oozy sound again, far away in front of him. The spaniel whined and was angrily kicked. Damn the dog, he ought to have learned sense by now!

Wind rising. No more twilight. Only faint moonlight now. Time to go. A noise of wings and black wedges circling in against the spaces of the clouds. Bang! Bang! He fired both barrels. One splash in front. A clamour away there, a frenzied shout: "Who are you, who are you?" a sharp shot, a scream.

Silence! A splash in the mere. Not a sound. Timmy howled. Not a sound. Yes, a splashing like hurried footsteps, faint in the distance. "My God," he said, in a strange voice that echoed in his ears. He tried to shout but his mouth was dry and rough and he merely croaked. He scooped up water, swallowed it and shouted: "Henderson! Henderson!" The noise seemed to fill the whole air, but it died in the night. "Henderson!" again he shouted, and knew there would be no reply. The trees shook. Clouds came over the moon and spots of rain fell. The mere was hardly visible now. What horror was over there? He clenched his teeth. He must go.

There was a punt below his feet, but it was full of water and useless. He left his tree and almost fell into the water-filled barrel which long ago had been a hiding-place for duck-shooters. His gun dropped and he picked it up again. He took his torch out and switched it on to guide himself along the neck of bog which led to the mainland: its arc illuminated tufted rushes, little pits of mud, stones, peaty pools, moths,

and pointed silver beads of rain. Then some impulses
of caution, almost like a voice crying in his ear, made
him switch it off again, and he scrambled rapidly along
the familiar bank in the rain, with now and then a
plunge to the knees in mud and now and then a trip
over a curling tree-root. At the western angle of the
mere, he stopped, stared into the semi-darkness and
listened again. The rain pattered heavily. No trace of
a glare was visible from the east where the fair was. A
tree creaked. "Wants greasing," he said aloud, not
meaning to speak. Then, "I'd better go on. I hope to
God he's only wounded. I want company!" and
laughed, without amusement, at his brutal humour.
Then on in the rain, now with white marks on trunk
and stone to guide him, up the slow stream, over the
plank, past the willows, through the rushes, until the
thorn-bushes filled the sky in front of him. It rained
pitilessly now and he was soaked through. But he
came to the last corner, and then, stooping, turned on
his torch and step by step approached Henderson's
lurking place. The spaniel flopped ahead, whimpered,
and stood still. At one step nothing was visible but
rain and the plants of the bog: at the next the mild rays
fell full on the prone plump body of the man. He lay
with his legs apart, his arms wide, his hands crisped,
his head back, his mouth open. There was a dark stain
on the left breast of his shooting jacket and below it—
of all things on God's earth—was a dead mallard,

beautiful in death though its gay colours were sobered in that light. The spaniel, obedient to his instincts, retrieved the bird and brought it to his master. Moorhouse stared at the picture like a lunatic: he trembled, his lips and teeth seemed beyond his control, he could hardly hold his gun. Then he laughed in a high voice, and "My bird, I think," he stammered. Then, "Don't be a fool," he quavered: then addressing himself sternly, "You've never lost hold over yourself before, Richard Moorhouse, and you'd better not do it now. There's this dead man and here are you. What's to be done?" With an effort he knelt and examined the body. No, never a gun shot, of course. It never sounded like it. A round bullet-hole. But no revolver in the dead man's hand, and not a sign of one on the boggy soil round about. He stood upright, and put out the torch. "I can switch it on whenever I like," he said, as though challenging the dead, and the elements, and some indefinable presence that mocked him. He clicked it on, stared at the body to steady himself, and was about to click it off again when he caught sight of something small and white on the bush to his left, and something at its foot. He reached for it, examined it, put it in his breeches pocket, stared at the dead again, and turned away. Then once more he turned, took the duck from the spaniel's mouth, and threw it out to the nearest clump of reeds. Once more he paused, and moved the torchlight-ray over the ground. He picked up Henderson's gun and opened it: yes, it was loaded. Darkness again. A risky game, but it had better be done. He fired both triggers. The reports sounded like cannon-shots, but the sounds died, and no distant shout followed them. He ejected the cartridges at Henderson's feet, and laid the gun down again.

He had no need of the torch now, and so constant a will o' the wisp had better not be seen wavering over those sodden lands. First mark the willows. Second mark the biggish tree. Third mark the white post. Fourth mark the hummocks. He had known them all from boyhood, and knew also to a minute the quarter of an hour which would take him, rain or no rain, to pass them all and reach the copse where they had left the car. Well, footprints wouldn't be good on that boggy waste at the best of times, and with rain like this they could look as long as they liked. A good thing his clothes had been soaked in the afternoon. He had gone a quarter of his distance, now groping, now running when, ahead of him, he heard a car start with a grinding of gears, run a little way, change up and change again and moan away in the distance towards the south. He smiled to himself acidly: "As a magistrate, I suppose I ought to go to the police. But in the circumstances it would be better not to. I've a revolver licence, apart from anything else . . . shut up you fool, what are you talking to yourself for . . . Henderson, Henderson, Henderson, Henderson.

Henderson, dead, dead, dead, dead, dead, dead, dead, dead, dead, dead, dead, dead, duck—a duck, duck—a—duck, duck—a—duck. Wanting to yell, he set his jaws tight and closed his fists on his gun, steering his course now by a far cottage light behind pine-trees which had come into sight over a slight rise. The ground fell again and he plunged into a pool of the stream, his splash echoed by another splash. "Pike," he said, "strange how they get here: but it is the spawn on the birds' legs, of course."

He reached the lightless car at last, and looked at his watch. "It must be about midnight," he thought: it was only seven. "Good Lord, if it had been midnight the servants'd have been back at the Manor again," he thought: then cursing because he was tired and wet and must not take the car, left the car behind him and trudged off. There was a mile and a half of winding road, first bare, then thickly arched over with trees: an unpleasant walk, in rain, wind and darkness at the best of times. When nearly home he heard steps approaching and his heart thumped hard. Suppose it was a policeman with one of those damned lanterns. He picked up the spaniel and held it and his gun close up to his body on the hedgeward side. A shapeless figure drew near and passed with a labourer's good night. Something prompted him to reply in a foreign accent, thick and guttural, and he heard the man stop as though he were looking round, and then

plod on. "And leaves the world to darkness and to
me," came into his head. A few hundred yards more
and there was the back entrance where there was no
lodge, and the old avenue of elms, and the Manor
House, a huddle of shadows, and the garage. Yes, the
Hendersons' car was in the next stall. He walked into
the garage, turned on the light and put his hand on
the bonnet, and smiled ironically: then he drew the
doors to, and stole round, avoiding the gravel, to the
front of the house. In one second-floor window shone
a light. It was Mrs. Henderson's. Moorhouse opened
the front door noiselessly, and walked down the hall
and got rid of his outer coverings, and turned on the
light in the library. He threw a glance round the
accustomed files of leather-backed books. "Looks
damned ordinary," he said. He filled a tumbler half
full of whisky and drank it neat. Then he walked up
to the Georgian mirror which ran the length of the
low mantelpiece and stared at his own face. It was
white and drawn, the eyes bright in deep sockets, the
lines from nostril to mouth cut deep, the moustache
and beard dank. He watched his mouth as he spoke.
"A damned interesting position," he said: then added,
less deliberately, "provided they don't take too long
finding him. That would be trying." Then a thought
flashing across his mind, he walked out into the hall.
"Quite," he observed, as he picked up an open note
which was lying on the largest of the chests: "To

Harry and Sir Richard: I was so tired after our day's walking that I've gone to bed. I've had all I want to eat. Don't wake me; Gladys."

But he thought he heard her moving about upstairs. And then he thought he heard crying and the voice of a comforter. He crept upstairs, feeling like a cowardly spy, and listened. "I wish you hadn't, oh, I wish you hadn't," he heard in Mrs. Henderson's voice; and then the determined mumbling of that woman, the companion. It was enough; he slunk downstairs again. In his own house! Biting his lip, he took Mrs. Henderson's note into the library and watched it drop to ashes in the fire. He went through the library into the study, where he kept rods, guns and account books, cleaned his barrels and restored the gun to the leather case which held its twin. His initials were stamped on it, "R. M." "Rotten Mess . . . Rank Madness," he said: and then wondered why strain should make people talk rubbish aloud. Very deliberately he pressed the spring of a panel cupboard in the wall, drew from one pocket a muddy handkerchief and put it in, and then from another something wrapped in a larger handkerchief. "Let's hope we shan't need them," he said.

He returned to the library, stared at his shadow on the wall, poured out another whisky and sat down in a deep leather chair before the fire. At what stage ought he to get worried about Henderson's disquieting non-

appearance? Over and over again he reconsidered the
events of the evening and his own position. It was
obvious that he must get alarmed some time, and
equally obvious that he had better not be precipitant.
The clock whirred and struck nine. If only those
damned servants would return his mind wouldn't
dwell so much on ringing up the Titbury police!
There was a soft knock at the door. He sprang up,
leant against the mantelpiece with his face to the door,
and said "Come in" with visions of policemen flashing
across his brain. It was Harbutt, the butler, plump,
cheerful and courteous, but abnormal in a smart lounge
suit. "Oh, you, Harbutt," remarked his master,
stifling a sigh of relief, "I thought you were all at the
fair."

"So we were, Sir Richard, but some of us 'ave come
'ome. Sick of the weather. The rest of 'em's in a
cinema."

"Is there a maid with you?"

"Yes, Sir Richard, Lucy—Simpson that is. And
Banks and myself."

"Banks hasn't gone off, I hope?"

"No, Sir Richard, 'e's down warmin' 'imself in the
kitchen."

"I may want him to drive the Daimler."

"Nothing wrong, I 'ope, Sir Richard?" He thought
his master's face looked odd.

"No, I hope not, Harbutt, but Mr. Henderson isn't

back and I'm worried about it. And I believe I heard
Timmy outside. Mr. Henderson went off in the
Chrysler by himself to the duck-pond, and took the
dog with him."

"What, our car, sir?"

"Yes, Mrs. Henderson said she might want theirs
to run over and see her mother, though in the end
she went to bed instead. He ought to have been back
two hours ago. He knows the way well enough, but
it's damned dark and if he loses his way and collapses
he might get rheumatic fever." He gave a little laugh.
"We don't want to lose our Member, do we, after
taking so much trouble to get him in?"

Harbutt gave an old servant's deferential laugh.
"No, Sir Richard. But Banks and I will find him in no
time. It's only a matter of shouting and a lantern."

"He may not answer if he is too far gone, you
know."

"We'll cover the ground all right, Sir Richard."

"If you don't find him ring me up."

"Yes, Sir Richard, and I will tell Lucy to put a
kettle on." He bowed and closed the door. After five
minutes there was the roar and dwindling hum of a
departing car.

*   *   *   *   *

In the morning, after that sleepless night of tramp-
ings, excited servants, and bustling policemen, and the

ultimate silence of dawn, since rent by screams from
upstairs, he received a message from the companion
saying that they must be driven over at once to Mrs.
Henderson's mother at Oakhanger, her mistress being
unfit to stay in the house any longer. Moorhouse felt
a strong revulsion against seeing them off the premises,
but, with the servants watching, he thought he had
better. His solicitude, as Mrs. Henderson heavily
muffled was helped along the hall by her woman, was
thrown away. The widow of the murdered man never
lifted her head, bowed in a stillness of grief that drew
murmurs of pity from Harbutt and the chauffeur; but
the stern, stony face of the maid, fiery dark eyes and
tight mouth, was turned full at him as she disclaimed
his aid with a movement of her free arm. "Thank
you," she said, "we can look after ourselves"; and
then, with a faint ironic smile, "and I hope you can
look after *your*self." Of her feelings and intentions
towards himself he was uncertain, but her almost
passionate concern for her stricken mistress was evident in every movement. Relieved to be able to stand
aloof, he watched them depart from the steps, wondering at the predicaments in which human beings find
themselves, at the secrets they carry about in their
breasts, musing on the passions of the wronged, the
desperate unscrupulousness of the frightened, the
general inability of men and women to see their affairs
in a due proportion, having regard to time and space,

the awful tale of forgotten years, the movements of land and sea, the uncountable wars and plagues of the past, the vast and remote processions of the stars and nebulæ. Yet, he reflected, as the closed car rolled off and he turned again to his room, he could hardly be expected to be immune from the general human frailty, and his own preservations and comfort, however momentary in the light of the eternities, were of some importance to him. It occurred to him then— for he was honest with himself—that he was, on the whole, a chivalrous man, though his generally ironic, even cynical, manner effectively disguised it from all except the penetrating: and that this indefensible habit of secrecy might well be useful to him.

*   *   *   *   *

It was after dinner a week later. The inquest had been adjourned. He had given his evidence, a candid and straightforward account of the dead man's movements, and his own. It was, up to a point, a very simple story. Henderson had insisted on trying the pond in the evening. He had gone as far as the garage with him, but felt very tired and excused himself to his guest, who had gone on with the car and spaniel— which had found its way home later. He had returned to the house and had never moved outside it until the news that the body had been found reached him. Pressed, very courteously, for further material evidence as to the commission and motive of the crime, he had said he was completely in the dark. The technical evidence ruled out suicide: the bullet was of a common type: no pistol had been found, which was not surprising with a large and muddy lake at hand. Nothing which looked like the faintest clue appeared at the inquest except that a labourer produced a vague statement about having passed a man who spoke with a foreign accent in a dark lane near the Manor. Witness could not say whether the man was carrying a gun, but could swear he was not followed by a dog: the solicitor privately apologised to Moorhouse for being compelled to ask absurd questions which might seem to hint in his direction.

"Your questions were quite proper, but I am afraid your apology is not," Moorhouse had said with a quick smile which relieved his worried neighbour, who once a year was asked to shoot. The foreign accent offered the one faint gleam of hope, and the newspapers "understood" that inquiries were being made in South Africa, where it was believed the dead man had made enemies. Mrs. Henderson might still throw light on the mystery, but she was, for the moment, ill from shock. The maid, Mrs Rose, gave formal evidence: she knew nothing about Mr. Henderson's affairs, having been with the family only three months. It was believed by the press that the business associates of the "shot M.P." might be of assistance; one of them told a reporter that a year ago he had heard Henderson muttering something about "blackmail" after receiving a cable from somewhere abroad. For the rest, there had not been a hint, except that a few of the more enterprising newspaper gossipers had thought fit to keep the name and record of Sir Richard Moorhouse before the public. "Just in case, I suppose," he reflected with a downward droop of the bearded lips, as he noticed casual paragraphs in which sympathy with him led by an easy transition to accounts of his pedigree, birth and education, his brief marriage to "a beautiful but delicate wife who died at Titford Manor," and innocent references to him as "a great reader, with a particular penchant for criminology," "a keen student of nature," "a fine shot," "a noted pedestrian," "at one time much sought after as an amateur actor," and a "world traveller who might, in 1908, have met in Johannesburg (where he stayed for several months) the young prospector, Henry Henderson, whose path crossed his so tragically twenty years after." Near, but not too libellously adjoining, the latest of these paragraphs he noticed an interesting reference to the "only peer ever hanged for murder," the mad Earl Ferrers, who murdered his servant, and went proudly to his death clad in white silk and riding in his private coach. What was to prevent anybody from wondering whether the Law wouldn't add a baronet to its gruesome bag? Nothing obviously: but he thought he had done his best so far to avert the calamity, and if he had to play his last card he had to play it—or rather the next to the last, for the last of all he shrank from contemplating. Conscience spoke with an uncertain voice, or rather with several conflicting voices.

It was half-past nine. He was in the library in his dinner jacket, stretched in a chair, smoking a cigar and reading, as detachedly as he was able, a volume on *Circumstantial Evidence*. As he read, his heart beat violently at certain cases and conclusions. The book was on his knees and he was ruminating on the extent to which the externally self-controlled among men may be tremulously emotional within, when the butler, pleased that his master should be visited by an old friend and evening companion, complacently announced Major French. French had been at school with him and lived near; but he also happened to be Chief Constable of the County.

There was a slightly feverish cordiality in French's greeting as he entered, with "How d'ye do, Dick? You don't mind my calling at this hour, do you, and in these clothes? No, no, it's not too hot. This chair will do perfectly. Well, emm, I don't know . . . perhaps . . . well, yes, a small spot of whisky."

"Almost refused my drink," thought Moorhouse, acutely conscious of a barrier, and observing that French, slightly frog-like with his round face and plump waistcoat and hips, was sitting on the edge of his chair. He brought his guest the glass of whisky, and looked him right in the eyes. "Does he see," he thought, as he mustered a frank and friendly expression, "a glaze of defence and hypocrisy in my eyes also?"

"You must need it," he said aloud, "I expect this wretched case is giving you an awful amount of trouble. I'm damned glad you've come, it's the first normal thing that's happened here for a week."

French took a large draught and looked round the room, challenged his host with his eyes and said:

"Look here, Moorhouse—Dick—I don't want you to be under any misapprehension. It's about this case that I've come to talk to you. There's nobody within earshot, I suppose?"

"Not unless you have a guard of police outside," said Moorhouse. The Chief Constable winced slightly.

"I happen to have two men with me in the ordinary way, but they have no instructions to eavesdrop. I have come to you as an old friend."

"You mean," said Moorhouse jocularly, "that nothing I say will be used in evidence against me!"

"There is no charge against you. I've merely come to you privately to see if you have anything to add to what you said before."

"Are you sure you are doing the correct thing in giving me what almost sounds like a warning?"

o

"You can leave me to decide upon that. I have other duties too. Ethel was my cousin, after all" (Moorhouse felt sick at the mention of his dead wife), "and you and I have been on terms of friendship for many years."

Words flashed across Moorhouse's brain: "Yes, you little blighter, you were my fag, and I wangled this job for you, and you always come to me to pour out your tribulations and my whisky. Oh, you're not so bad in your way, but you are insufferably stupid." Almost simultaneously he said:

"Look here, Ted, be frank with me, what is it that is troubling you?" French thawed at the warmth of the accustomed atmosphere, walked over and helped himself to another drink in the old way, and almost forgot his suspicion.

"I'm glad you're making it easy for me, Dick. The fact is you may be having an awkward time ahead of you. Of course you know very well that I myself should never dream that you, of all people, could have anything to do with, er . . ."

"A murder, you mean. I should damn well think not."

"You're quite right. Now, let's talk it over sensibly. You understand, I daresay, that what we're talking about is not what your old friends know, but evidence."

"And evidence is a curious thing, of course. Fire away."

"Well, we've been working at this case and we've got nowhere, nowhere at all."

"And you're back at the Manor."

"Not to put too fine a point on it, we are. You see," French went on in his old confiding way, forgetting for the time whom he was talking about, "we have to follow any clue that is offered to us, and . . ."

"Let me tell you once and for all, Ted, that you can discuss this case as if it didn't involve me at all. Look here, I'll save you embarrassment. I'll outline the whole bloody thing myself, if you like!"

French squirted from a syphon into his glass.

"I wish you would," he said.

"Very well. Mr. Henry Henderson, M.P. an unpleasant man of doubtful antecedents, with an ill-treated wife . . ."

"Who said she was ill-treated?"

"I did. But never mind. She at least would never be suspected by anyone. At all events this malodorous, though virile and energetic man, was staying, in his capacity as chosen of the electorate, with Sir Richard Moorhouse at Titford Manor. Is that all right?"

"Oh, of course it is."

"On a certain evening of November 1928, Mr. Henderson was found dead by Sir Richard Moorhouse's duck-pond. Two dead duck accounted for the discharge of his gun barrels and he had obviously been killed by a pistol shot fired by another hand."

"That's all right so far as it goes," said French, looking vacantly, glass in hand, into the great fire of logs.

"Obviously, and perhaps I can skip the rest of the obvious. The question is, who did it?"

"Of course, who did it?"

"Now the first certainty is that it must have been done either by somebody who went to the duck-pond with Mr. Henderson or by somebody who was following his movements, tracked him closely there, for the night was dark and the path difficult, and shot him. It is admitted by Sir Richard Moorhouse that he started for the duck-pond with Mr. Henderson and a spaniel. But Sir Richard states that he only went as far as the garage, that he sent the spaniel on with Mr. Henderson, and that the spaniel returned alone later in the evening. For all this there is no evidence but his own word: the servants were all out. Mrs. Henderson and her companion were upstairs, as he agrees. For the moment we return to the other supposition: that some person unknown with some motive unknown for killing him had been lurking in the neighbourhood for some days."

"Not necessarily for some days," interjected French, the sense of evidence strong in him.

"Well, probably for some days, as the best of opportunities would probably not occur on the night of this stranger's arrival. However, it is immaterial. If we assume the stranger, we must ask ourselves whom Henderson may have injured, and who would have so strong a motive for revenge against him as to plan his deliberate murder."

"Yes," French muttered.

"The obvious place to look, especially after that rather sketchy statement of the man who heard a foreign accent, was South Africa. Enemies could certainly be traced there, but—this I assume without knowledge—all those who could be identified were either dead or in jail."

"Yes, confound it!" said French.

"The jail-birds wouldn't speak; the dead couldn't; the woman he lived with couldn't be traced."

"How did you know that?" exclaimed French, with a sudden shrewd look in his eye.

"Oh," replied Moorhouse, flicking off the ash of his cigarette, "I didn't know: I merely guessed it. Persons of his kidney have always lived with women and have always deserted them. Poor creature! I bet she had the hell of a time with him. A man like that would be enough to drive a woman mad! However, the plain truth is that Africa yielded you nothing, and you came back here. And coming back here, you—I mean, of course, your colleagues—have been unable to restrain a certain amount of curiosity about myself—shared, I may say, by the newspapers—though they are diffident about saying so."

"I wish you wouldn't talk so wildly," said French. "It's very uncomfortable for me, and you ought to know that I wish you well out of this."

"I assure you," replied Moorhouse, "that I am not in the least wild, and you know it. You know, moreover, that, having returned to the consideration of myself, you discovered certain facts that might tend, if supported, to suggest that I went to the duck-pond with Henry Henderson, that I crept round upon him in the dark, and that I shot him, and left him, and then stole home by unfrequented ways."

"We've got a few facts. They don't amount to much one way or the other. I never said you did it. It's ridiculous."

"Nothing could be more ridiculous," said Moorhouse, now pacing up and down before the fire, and shooting continual keen glances at his old fag, "but it is not for the police to rule hypotheses out, is it? Remember what virtuous people have committed murder—professors, clergymen, retired colonels, Sunday-school teachers, suburban violinists! Why not a widower baronet, for a change? Especially as he had frequently been heard to say that the world would be much better off without swine like Henderson in it."

"I never said you said that."

"No, but I did, often; and you've got it all down in little note-books; and I say it again, and you can take it down again, if you like. But this of course isn't the most important thing, is it?"

"I don't quite know what you mean."

"My dear Chief Constable, you have a perfectly sound glimmering of what I mean, though you can hardly conceive that you are right, or that I should have the audacity to mention it."

"I don't know, all the same," said French, obstinately, not without betraying in his expression the hope of learning something new.

"No," said Moorhouse, with a sudden access of energy, "I'm not telling you anything you don't know already. There's nothing to tell. I'm merely referring to your discovering that one of my pistols is missing."

"How the devil——"

"Naturally I was not left uninformed that your police had paid me a little call when I was well known to be off the premises. One of the pistols has gone!"

"That's the deuce of it!" said French—and Moorhouse felt a slight renewed affection for him, as it became clear that he had tried to shirk or rebut this evidence in his own mind. "Where is it?"

"If I knew where it was," cried Moorhouse impatiently, "we shouldn't be having all this bother.

I suppose somebody's been cleaning it, and left it somewhere."

"But," said French, more stiffly, "your butler saw you showing it to the whole Henderson family only the day before."

"What!" said Moorhouse quietly, but in surprise. "You mean that Harbutt said that? Harbutt? Oh, all right, it's true enough. I suppose he was quite right to tell the truth. Lies in these affairs always get found out."

"You're right enough there," French observed, "we're pretty well accustomed to lies, and know the sound of them."

"Well," Moorhouse went on, "you don't suppose, Ted, that I've been telling lies to-night, do you?"

"I believe every word you say," said French, "but it's ugly all the same. What about what that companion was overheard to say to Mrs. Henderson when she was getting her into the car here?"

"Whatever it was, it's news to me," replied Moorhouse boldly. "Who heard it?"

"My men—and your servants, I suppose."

"What did she say?"

"Very little, but a jury might think it had great significance. It was, 'Oh, Sir Richard! Oh, Sir Richard!'"

"That's not much from an hysterical woman, is it?"

"Possibly not, possibly it is, or a jury might think so. We have often got clues from hysteria. She might have said more if that companion of hers hadn't shut her up."

"Yes, the dragon," said Moorhouse. "I suppose I ought to be obliged to her, even if she has got the stony face of a Medusa. But listen to me now. What does all this amount to?"

"How can I tell what a jury might think, or what further clues mightn't turn up? Of course, I take your word for it you're innocent; but even if there isn't enough to go on, you're not going to escape suspicion."

"And it isn't going to leave me, eh? A pleasant prospect!"

"It isn't much. You'd be all right with a decent alibi," said French, fencing with his eyes.

"Not always procurable," sighed Moorhouse, "even by the least guilty of men."

The telephone rang in the adjoining study. "Excuse me a moment," said Moorhouse, "I was expecting an answer to a message, and this is probably it." He passed through the folding doors, left them open and spoke in the dark in full hearing of his visitor:

"Yes . . . Is that Mrs. Rose? . . . Yes . . . I'm very sorry . . . Oh, yes, I found it and I've got it! . . . It was rather careless, you know . . . A man

must protect himself. Can't be helped . . . I think
so . . . In the last resort, but it has to be . . . Good
night . . . I hope she's better."

When he returned to the library—once more to
press a drink upon the willing French—his face wore
a look both anxious and determined. He paced up
and down the room with quick strides, and then,
facing French squarely, said quietly: "I've been telling
you lies."

French was proud of his equilibrium as a policeman,
and his plump face assumed a supercilious expression.
"So I have observed all the time," he said.

"Very penetrating of you," said Moorhouse. "I
suppose you imagine that I am going to say that I
was there when Henderson was murdered?"

French flushed and stammered: "I don't see why
you should . . . I mean . . ."

Moorhouse's mouth drooped in an acid smile.
"Never mind; at any rate you will be relieved. Your
people need hardly go further with their conjectures.
I have just been authorised to disclose my alibi."

"But you said you were here," said French.

"So I was," replied Moorhouse, "with Mrs.
Henderson."

There was a pause.

"Oh, I see," said French lamely, "you sent him
out because you were in love with his wife."

"No," remarked Moorhouse, shrinking from the

suggestion, "don't take it too seriously. This isn't one of those intrigues that end in marriage."

French rose, helped himself abstractedly to a cigarette, and muttered that he must be going. Then he added, half-heartedly, "What witness had you?"

"Oh," said Moorhouse, "her maid was about. They are very thick with each other."

"I'm sorry, Dick," said French. "The last thing I wanted to do was to embarrass you. But there is one thing still, you know."

"Well?" asked Moorhouse.

"The pistol."

"Oh, that's easy enough! Forgive me a moment, will you?" Moorhouse went into the study, opened the cupboard, took out a pistol in a handkerchief, carefully wiped it with the handkerchief and brought it into the library. "There she is!" he said jocularly.

"But why didn't you produce this before," asked French.

"My dear boy, simply because I wanted to test your faith in me."

"We've got our duty to do," mumbled French shamefacedly.

"Yes, I know you have. It was damned brutal of me. But I'm not quite myself. You've never been suspected of a murder. 'Pon my word, I don't believe you ever will be! Sorry, old boy," he said.

"Oh, you're just the same as ever," laughed French, finishing his drink.

He showed French out and returned to the library.

"Extraordinary," he said to himself, "that that woman Rose could have been with the Hendersons for three months and that he should never have found out that his wife knew who she was . . . Poor devil . . . But he got what he deserved . . . It was rather stupid of me not to guess the right one at the start, but it hardly mattered which of his two women put him out of the world."

WHAT MIGHT HAVE HAPPENED

WHAT MIGHT HAVE HAPPENED

(*Being extracts from the Diary of Alfred Crooke, Leader-writer on the staff of the* Daily Argus, *a newspaper of intemperate temperance views.*)

1918.—*Feb.* 2. Went down to the House. House and Press Gallery crowded. Heard Prime Minister's announcement that total Prohibition must be adopted for the duration. Firmly, though sympathetically, explained that waste of men and material could no longer be permitted. Existing stocks to be reserved for troops. Contents of private cellars to be retained by owners, but not replenished. Stocks of clubs and pubs to be taken over at valuation. No drinking in public. Leaders of all parties supported measure, and gave solemn pledges to public that it would be purely temporary and Peace would at once bring *status quo*. Feel uneasy. This looks as though measure would be permanent. After debate had drinks in Gallery Bar. Everybody there, at once gloomy and excited. At night wrote leader warmly welcoming temporary chance of Great Experiment. Wish we had more at home.

Feb. 3. Pubs closed to-day. Curious atmosphere all

over City, especially in Fleet Street. Sort of hectic merriment as though a new and astonishing game were being played. Had no idea so many of my friends possessed hip-pocket flasks. Called at "Green Cow" and four other places. Pressure already felt. Only known customers served, and those furtively. Others told place not open. "Wot, me serve cocoa?" asked old Wiggins.

Feb. 4. Duke of Middlesex dramatically drank water in public for the first time in his life.

Feb. 10. The editor has given me a case of whisky to fortify me when writing my leaders. He was very strict in his injunctions as to my keeping it dark. Our proprietor was always liable to enter. I had just put it into my cupboard when Sir Elisha walked in. He congratulated me on my leaders. "Well, well, Mr. Crooke," he said, "we may live to see England a teetotal country yet." I began impetuously and indiscreetly, "But the vast majority of the male population . . ." Happily, with his usual complacency, he interrupted: "You are quite right; the vast majority of the male population are already perceptibly better off. By the end of the year it will be impossible for any statesman to repeal this beneficent measure. I must ask you a blunt question," he added.

"I will answer anything you ask, Sir Elisha," I said.

"Were you a consumer of alcohol before Prohibition was introduced?" was his question.

"To a very moderate extent I was," I replied.

"I am glad you have answered me candidly," he said. "I am perfectly aware that there were very few teetotalers in Fleet Street. But do you not already feel a better, more clear-minded and more active man, because of the deprivation of your wonted stimulant?"

"Indeed I do, Sir Elisha," I replied. He left the room with a smile of triumph, probably to report my conversion to the Editor; I took a stiff peg of the Editor's whisky out of the bottle.

July 18. It rather looks as though the War now will be only a matter of months, and even weeks. Really remarkable how Prohibition Law has been obeyed. Rumours of all sorts of secret dives where drink sold at exorbitant prices, but must say most of my friends Denying Selves with enthusiasm worthy of Salvation Army. What is use of having law if don't obey it?

July 19. Reggie Akenside came in, cheery as usual. Recovered from wound but likely to have long leave. Persuaded me to come to Soho where he has a favourite drinking resort. Went and found an Italian restaurant. People eating and drinking coffee, etc., downstairs. Upstairs with proprietor to bedroom with sink in it where blowsy wife washing glasses. Proprietor took off coat and mixed cocktails. Gin tasted strange: Akenside says they're making it at home.

P

Suspect methylated spirit, but no proof. Back to office, where wrote leader pointing out physical and moral improvement in people since Devil of Drink exorcised. Only wish change could be made permanent "of course after proper consultation of people." Jack Jones made jokes about Prohibition in House: Lady Astor indignant.

August 3. War seems won. Is liquor situation relaxing? For months now have seen no one drinking except at home, in office, in illicit pubs, etc., etc. But breaches now becoming more open, it appears. Akenside, promoted Captain, but still free from duties (a jolly good soldier, too), dragged me out to lunch. "What do you want to *work* for?" in his cheery way. Took me to strange club with some name like Junior Reform at back of Charing Cross, for cocktails. Here, at this time of day, numbers of officers, lizards and young women dancing in crowded small room flat-iron shaped, with big pursy young Jew playing piano and his brother looming round as actual waiter and potential Chucker-Out. "Four large Martinis, Isidore," said Akenside to this bruiser. "Certainly, Mr. Akenside," said he, with a glance at me. "Mr. Crooke is all right!" remarked my fair-haired boy. "Just you give him whatever he wants whenever he comes in!" Drinks dubious. I asked Mr. Isidore where he got his ingredients from. "All old stuff, sir; all old stuff," he replied evasively.

Politicians of all parties, on all sorts of occasions except debates in House, suspiciously congratulating country on magnificent response to law. Already noting improvement in Output, Physique of Young, etc. Snaggs very strong on this yesterday at Reigate.

August 4. Lunch with Tooker in Brook Street. Met Snaggs for first time. Appeared to be drunk before lunch. No doubt of appearance after lunch. Talked freely about prospects of Post-War Prohibition. "Drink all ri' f'r me an' you, ol' f'lah, but workin' man can't carry it. Manufacturers all 'gree. Wa' we wan' one law f'r rich, 'nother f'r poor." I observed that I was not rich. "No, no, no," he said, "but genelman, genelman; come shame shing."

September 5. Late in the evening Akenside came in with young soldier on leave, candidate for Wapping, and took me to twelve Chinese places in Wapping where every kind of drink obtainable at monstrous prices, but perfect order and quiet prevailing. Asked Bolton (the young candidate) whether police ignorant. Replied that police interfered only if disorder or crooked conduct: "and very sensible too." I quite agree with that; and strongly disagree with leader I wrote just before demanding that efforts of small minority to evade salutary law should be, as Lady

Astor suggests, vigorously dealt with. Akenside made strange suggestion: "Why don't you make wine at your week-end cottage?" If the War goes on, will this law result in wine being made wholesale in England as it never has been since the Middle Ages and the Monks? Rather romantic! Lynchets on Wiltshire downs might as well be vine-terraces as corn-terraces. I did hear a rumour that a sub-editor in the office was pressing grapes on Sundays at Herne Bay.

October 12. This situation about liquor is really rather absurd. As far as I can see much more money is being spent on it than ever was, and the public gets much less for its money, but the much less rots more intestines than ever were rotted in the good old days. Sir Elisha very pleased with my leader yesterday pointing out that coffee, cocoa and tea stimulate without deleterious after effects. At home Ethel delighted, having discovered from friend at Women's Institute some strange formula for making rum from sugar in kitchen boiler.

November 11. Peace declared. Prohibition lapses. But does it? Must look up order under D.O.R.A. to see if date given. Editor gave whole office champagne.

November 12. No date. So far as I can see things can remain indefinitely. Sir Elisha came in instructing me to say nothing about Prohibition until subject becomes live issue. He had just seen his close confederate Snaggs who tells him that one more year will establish the thing for ever. Wrote leader on Polish Corridor.

December 21. Reported general riots of demobilised troops at not finding facilities for celebration on return. Instructed not say anything. English a docile race and will settle down.

1919.—*January* 18. John, leaving O.T.C., has gone to Oxbridge (Corpus) to-day. My only son: the new generation. So far as I know he has never tasted liquor. Perhaps he never will. Akenside called, strongly urging me to say nothing about Drink Question. "This from you!" I exclaimed. The cheerful lad then gave me to understand that having a gratuity of £500 or so (after all debts to waiters and stewards paid), and having no wish to join Polish or Mexican armies, he had gone into partnership with his two large Jewish friends at the Junior Reform Club and started business as what the Americans (I believe) call a Bootlegger. Would not divulge sources of supply, but I gather that arrangements are already made for resumption of old South Coast smuggling and that Irish potheen, already common, may shortly become commoner. Arrange take case of whisky a month from him, to be delivered by car at my Surrey cottage. Price horrible (£15), but what can one do? Wrote leader suggesting drink question better be postponed year or two, until public opinion settles down, and then possible Referendum.

January 19. Almost lost job! Sir Elisha rushed in furious at Referendum suggestion. I timidly observed that I had always thought he was a great apostle of the Referendum. He raged and stormed. I cringed. Offence not to be repeated. I now see his point. The Referendum may properly be applied to questions of which the populace knows nothing at all, but the populace must never be consulted on any matter concerning which it has both knowledge and an opinion of its own. Akenside called, sunny as usual: "I thought you'd like to know, old chap, I made £200 last week." He has found his métier at last.

January 25. Wish everybody wouldn't talk about Prohibition. Drink isn't boring, but talk about it is! Parliament reassembles. Will subject be raised?

January 26. Question to Snaggs by Jack Jones in House as to "Lifting of Drink Ban" (I quote evening paper). Snaggs replied, "The matter is under consideration by my department." Lady Astor: "So there!" Jack Jones: "Same to you, and many of them!" Wrote leader deploring vulgarity of Jack Jones.

January 29. Charming week-end at home in country —Bill and Emily, Robinsons, Tuckers and ourselves. Ethel sprung delightful surprise. Rum made in her own kitchen-boiler. This, with Akenside's usual whisky (now strongly Irish in flavour), gin from the laundry-man, and a bottle of port brought by Bill, made the occasion a great success. I was a little frightened about Ethel. If she were caught and convicted, Sir Elisha would sack me at once. She very reassuring. Says village policeman thinks law all rot and helped her in final distillation. Burden off mind. Thank Heaven for sensible and decent English police!

Memo., February 2, 1919.

Prohibition has now been in force for one year. What is the situation? The Upper Classes are, of course, all right. They have cellars, and when one dines with them one goes through the usual routine from the cocktails to the brandy, port, and stirrup-cup of whisky: nothing could be better than the dinner I had last night at Snaggs', who seems rather to have taken to me. Those who had not large cellars are, of course, paying heavily for new stuff, but they don't seem to mind: the extra excitement of the illicit seems to compensate for the extra expense. For the men of the middle classes numerous drinking dens, under various disguises (I had a whisky yesterday in the fitting-vault of a tailor's), have sprung up, and the men, at a price, obtain an approximation to what they want, though it is lamentable to see so many beer-drinkers turn into spirit drinkers. As Akenside remarked to me the other day: "You can now get a drink anywhere in London except at a pub." That is roughly true: those of the old inns which remain in business sell nothing but "soft drinks," being congenitally afraid of the police. Only one respectable club, that I know of, still sells cocktails to members whose guests are certain to be authentic: but there is a custom springing up in others of having locker-rooms (as in golf clubs) in which members store their own liquor, with counters on which white-coated barmen mix the desired drinks, breaking no law about sale.

As for the working classes, it is always difficult, in this country, to know *what* they are doing. I took a trip to Whitechapel last week and saw more drunk men in a night than I used to see in a year: they must have got drink somewhere, but I haven't the ghost of a notion where. Home-brewed or smuggled: those are the alternatives. Raw spirit, I believe, can be made quite cheaply from potatoes or even wood: and every ship that enters the Pool from the Continent carries brandy and the more potent liqueurs. Registrar-General's Report states deaths from alcoholism increased one hundred per cent in last year. Must write leader arguing that these only extreme cases. Can I use sentence, "Prohibition kills or cures?" Better not, perhaps: safety first! No doubt vast majority of population violently against Prohibition. Country districts solid. Yet such is allegiance to parties that few will desert on this one question. Ireland and Protection cut across everything. Almost all the politicians in tacit conspiracy to burke this question; unless big new Anti-Prohibition Party started British peasant has nobody to vote for—only a choice of evils. Everybody grumbles in trains, etc., but nobody can suggest a way out. Such is democracy!

May 2. John back at Oxbridge. Appears to have learnt a lot. Wrote leader early, ridiculing Jack Jones's new Anti-Prohibition Party, which has no support in House or Press. Got home to country and found Ethel on doorstep reminding me fifteenth anniversary of our wedding. Said I remembered; of course I didn't. But the darling! She'd got all the neighbours in to meet me, and they'd all brought bottles, and she herself had got especially for me—she wouldn't tell me whence—a bottle of Château Neuf du Pape, which she imagined to be my favourite drink simply because she remembered my ordering it once when we were first engaged. Oddly enough, it was the right stuff. Everybody except myself got rather drunk and reeled about.

June 6. Fall of Government. Snaggs formed new Coalition: universal suffrage, including women (let in, presumably, to reinforce Prohibition), and vigorous repression in Ireland, with Black-and-Tans greatly increased. Jack Jones, rising in rage, asked new Home Secretary if nothing was to be done about fulfilling old promises about abolishing Prohibition. Home Secretary, with hauteur, and amid general cheering, said he could not reply to questions so offensively couched. Jones, on rising to protest, shouted down. Dined at 10, Downing Street—nobody but Snaggs and Home Secretary. They wish keep in close touch with *Argus*. After brief soundings, champagne, etc., produced. General agreement Prohibition to be made permanent in interest of working classes and prosperity generally. Rather surprised to hear Home Secretary refer to my esteemed proprietor as "that humbug, Sir Elisha." Still more surprised to find Snaggs, getting confidential about sources of supply, recommending me Akenside as trustworthy bootlegger. I said I had known him since before the war, when he was a youth writing pretty but ineffective lyrics. Snaggs, with political-pontifical air, scrutinizing the light through his port, said, "That young man will go far!" Snaggs' fat face looking very heavy and flushed; eyes leered like a saurian's. On doorstep, affably saying good-bye, exhorted me to nail Prohibition banner to mast having put hand to plough. That's all right: Sir Elisha will see to that. Besides, where should I get employment if I had a row with *Argus?* Not a paper in London but either supports Prohibition or mysteriously ignores it—with the exception of Lord Otterburn's *Messenger* which recommends more drastic enforcement coupled with a special exception in favour of Empire Wines. Not if I know it! Remedy worse than disease!

November 5. Tremendous surprise! Snaggs and Co. have made treaty with Ireland giving full Dominion Rights. English troops and auxiliaries to be withdrawn.

November 6. Akenside, blooming and Astrakhan-collared, rushed into my room. "No more potheen," he cried, "the Irish will be able to make whisky openly as much as they like, and you'll get the right stuff now." "Haven't I been getting it hitherto?" I asked. He looked embarrassed.

December 9. Irish distilleries working full blast at whisky which must be described as "for unknown destination." Editor came into my room chuckling and said not a single Black-and-Tan had returned to England or was likely to.

1921.—*May* 1. This Prohibition business is getting on my nerves. Here is all Europe at sixes and sevens—

Reparations unsettled, Disarmament unsettled, the whole Peace of the World at stake—and one hears nothing from morn till night except Drink, Drink, Drink. The men in my carriage talk about it on the way up from Guildford, exchanging information about bootleggers and prices, and smacking their lips over last night's beverages; I hear nothing else at the office, or at lunch at the club, or at dinner if I dine out, or at home if people come in. Dodging the law has become a national game—with Akenside and his kin holding the bank! It is pouring in from Ireland and from every foreign country; it's pretty damnable, considering how uncorrupt our customs and police forces have been in the past, to reflect on the number of them (simply because they don't think the law coincides with morality or common sense) who must now be privy to smuggling and illicit dealing.

May 2. Week-end at home. An extraordinarily jolly party. Old Fraser, the farmer at Hurtley, rang me up and asked me if we would like to come to a wine-bottling party. It seemed an odd thing: recalling Provence and Italy, the Georgics, white oxen and the trampling of grapes. However, we said we'd go; and a strange party we found. We were late and they had already—old Fraser, the Vicar, and the local Sergeant of Police—gone down to the cellar to start operations. Fraser, when our car rolled up to the old dark house, came up the cellar steps with a horn lanthorn, and peered into our faces. Then he led us down a very much oak-beamed, peeling-whitewashed and cob-webbed staircase to a low-ceilinged cellar leading to another beyond. There they sat, the Vicar and the Policeman, by a huge barrel, complacent smiles—no, childish exaltation—on their faces—just the other side of the doorway which led from the first cellar to the second. "Try our others first," said Fraser. In the second cellar (for this shrewd old man had got to work early) there were bins labelled 1918 and 1919, not to mention sundry old bottles of Sherry, Bene-dictine, Port, Cointreau, etc., which were there to give this English Cellar body. We sampled the old vintages: not so bad: rather crude claret, but better than the best to us, having been made in England and in face of all the Snaggses and Sir Elishas! Then we set to. One drained the liquor out of the barrel by a syphon pipe, one held the bottle, one plied the corking machine, one stacked the finished product. "Hurtley, 1920": perhaps, in the future, it may be a "collectors' item." E. and I went home in proud possession of two full bottles of each year, including the current one.

May 3 (*Sunday*). To the office. Great Temperance Demonstration at Sheffield. Chairman of United Kingdom Alliance stated that alcoholic drinks had been virtually exterminated, and that within a few years nobody in England would know what they were. He himself had not seen a soul touching liquor for a year. Took a bottle of Akenside's best Irish out of cupboard and wrote pretty eloquent leader applauding all parties for leaving this prickly question to settle itself, calling attention to general improvement in public weal (though not to increase in alcoholic deaths, crime generally and shootings of police and smugglers in particular) and suggesting that present time of transition must inevitably lead to time of general abstemiousness, younger generation growing up entirely innocent of contact with deleterious liquids. Later, at club, met young Mackay, who took me off to night resort in Wardour Street where many young people of both sexes, noisy band and much drink. Preferred rustic quiet of "Dog and Partridge" in old days: nightly pot of beer and talk of crops, trees, cricket, changing customs and characters of local landlords.

June 15. Just back from Oxbridge, whither John (in freshers' enthusiasm) insisted that we should go. Marked change since my day. At College Ball no drinks: everything demure and everybody apparently waiting for something. Danced a little with casually introduced sisters and sweethearts, mostly rather bored by a man of my advanced age, and then John (and an effusive, and apparently opulent, young friend

called Cholmondeley) came up to Ethel and me, as
we sat in a marquee by the river eating ices, suggesting
that we might like to come to a little party they were
stealing off to. Ethel was stimulated by the suggestion:
she always likes to know what the young are doing:
and we all went to the gate together (hours of getting
in and out of college being this week suspended) and
got into a Bentley car which belonged to this young
Cholmondeley. We drove out of the town for two
miles or so and then came to a large house, "in its
own grounds," which had apparently been taken for
the occasion. Young Cholmondeley stopped at the
gate to speak to a policeman. "All right, Robert?" he
asked. "Yes, quite all right, sir," replied the policeman; and we drove up to the door. Inside there was
the most terrific din. Hundreds of undergraduates
(including, apparently, all the brains and beauty of
the University) streaming through all the ground-floor
rooms and up and down the big staircase. In the
largest room an incredibly rowdy jazz band and a
press of couples dancing, mostly with glasses full of
brown liquid in their hands. Many were swaying
threateningly; in the corners there were a few, of both
sexes, who had obviously "passed out." But what
surprised us most was the row of apparently unper-
turbed chaperones (mostly, I suppose, mothers) who
sat along the walls. I live a retired life. I knew that
Prohibition was not working; but I did not know that

it was failing to this extent. When we left at four everybody was drunk. To-night I wrote leader strongly supporting view that complete enforcement of Prohibition was now mere matter of time.

November 15 (*Saturday*). Akenside (a little fatter about the jowl) suddenly appeared at the cottage in Rolls-Royce, with exquisite lady alleged (and I take it, correctly) to be his wife. Affable introductions all round (Ethel, oddly enough, never met him in the old days when I used to knock about with him and listen to his amusing chatter), lunch, and then an hour with Akenside in my study. He began characteristically: "Look here, old thing, you were jolly good to me in the old days when I hadn't got a bean, and I want to do you a good turn now." The good turn took the form of an offer of "ground floor" shares in a concern called the Cork and Limerick Indigo Company. When I said I didn't know anything about indigo, he replied that indigo, in this case, was a cover for the smuggling of whisky—which, under the terms of the Treaty, could be made *ad lib.* in Ireland but not exported to England. I have never very seriously worried about the divergence between my practice and my preaching over this business. After all, a journalist (is he not?) is in the position of any advocate. He is paid to put a certain point of view, another journalist is paid to put another point of view, and the public is the judge. At actually putting money into smuggling, however, I did for some time baulk. In the end, when I was promised 1,000 per cent per annum for my money, I saw that there was another aspect to the matter, and I gave Akenside my cheque for £500. "I can promise you you won't regret it," he said: and off he hummed in his great car, with his fluffy wife—whom Ethel alleges (it hardly seems credible) not to realise at all how her husband makes his money.

Memo., Feb. 2, 1921.

Prohibition has now been in operation for three years. Grumbling is universal but nothing is done. "Universal" is correct: the majority grumble at Prohibition and a very vocal minority pass resolutions complaining that it is so badly enforced. No, there seems at least one completely cheerful and satisfied person. I take the following from this morning's *Daily Mail*:

PROHIBITION COMPLETE SUCCESS

F. C. C. PRESIDENT'S CONFIDENCE. NEW YORK, TUESDAY: Interviewed here to-day the President of the British Free Church Council, Dr. Snooper, declared that no great reform in history had been carried out with such thorough success as Prohibition in Britain. They must not believe the sensational newspapers which made so much capital out of a few scandals. The heart of the people was sound.

All Scotland now making whisky at home: all England beer and wine. Ireland incredibly prosperous: all taxes abolished except excise duty on whisky. Prohibition still not a real issue in our politics, Bolshevism and other red herrings cutting across. English strange placid people: will swallow anything, even methylated spirit.

February 3. Startling news to-day. Ulster in arms, declaring will fight England unless allowed to join Irish Free State. Reasons purely financial; temptation of single tax too great. (Later.) Snaggs announces immediate Bill giving up Ulster, and expresses delight that Union of Hearts is at last achieved in Ireland. Pressure now likely to be lightened by much greater imports of whisky from Belfast.

June 24. John back from 'Varsity, taking out hip-flask as cool as cucumber. Very sorry about this: I never touched a thing at his age: but what can one expect if you will forbid them to do what they think they've a right to do? At night went to London and wrote leader supporting Bishop of Battersea's contention that old topers slowly dying out and new bright-eyed generation growing up unused to poison of alcohol.

June 26 (*Saturday*). Terrific surprise to-day. Akenside has bought the Park: I am just outside his gates. He called (I will say as lively and free from side as ever) in a vast car with a chauffeur. Told me he'd made half a million and should retire at a million. Meanwhile was anxious for career of public service and was about to be adopted as candidate for this Division in succession to sitting member. "But I didn't know he had any intention of retiring!" I said. "He hadn't," remarked Akenside, "but he has now. Snaggs squared him." "What is your policy about liquor?" I asked. "Strongly in favour of leaving things as they are," said he. Well, I suppose things might be worse. At least we haven't got a large population of Sicilians, etc., such as they have in Chicago. I am rather proud of my country when I reflect on the way in which Prohibition has been made a dead letter. Hardly any shootings, or stealings at all: everything done quietly: either the smugglers go quietly or the police go quietly: and nothing is done in the way of raids except when some preternaturally active busy-body gets on the job.

November 8. Sensation to-day. Jopson, our member (and a really zealous "Dry"), arrested at Dover for smuggling brandy. Officials anxious to do their best, but what can be done when a trunk falls to the ground, bottles are smashed, brandy leaks out, and the Bishop of Battersea is standing by? He has been remanded and will certainly go to gaol and resign seat. Whole Press will fume with indignation to-morrow. My leader demands indignantly how people can be expected to obey law if responsible persons break it. Delightful evening with three old college friends, one of whom produced genuine bottle of French monks' Green Chartreuse. Never liked the beastly stuff until now, but what nectar it is now that it seems to come from a vanished world!

1922.—*January* 2. Jopson convicted after appeal. Resigned seat. Akenside adopted. Probably no contest at by-election.

January 3. No by-election either. Snaggs suddenly announced to-day must have General Election in order that country should express opinion about Iraq Mandate, just as it looked as though J. Jones and Lady Astor might work up a real struggle about Prohibition.

January 22. Everybody excited about Iraq. Prohibition forgotten. Akenside's Election Address out: statesmanlike document, only reference to drink being short blunt sentence pointing out beneficial effects of present law.

February 15. Eve of poll meeting. Akenside great success. Strong telegram from Snaggs recommending him. Towards end a rowdy at back of hall yelled out:

"You made your money out of bootlegging." Akenside splendid in retort: "I do not condescend to reply to accusations such as that and I appeal to my supporters to be chivalrous and not to treat that gentleman as he deserved." Man hurled from hall, minus coat, waistcoat, breeches and probably half his hair.

February 17. Akenside in easily. Huge majority for Snaggs and Iraq Mandate. Whoever had been returned we should have been told that there was a great majority for Law Enforcement. Jack Jones returned by vast majority for Silvertown: but remains only member of out-and-out party.

February 27. Small dinner at Downing Street. Half the Cabinet and a few of the more influential journalists. Mahogany, silver, and beautiful wines: at such moments one realises the strength and dignity of the traditions which have made this country what it is.

September 3. Sir Elisha, at last realising that the country is not as dry as he thought it was, has been talking seriously to me—meanwhile raising my salary by £300 a year as a small recognition of my efforts on behalf of The Great Cause. Says that some politicians and some papers secret enemies of Prohibition and even suspects police not wholly safe and perhaps one or two minor politicians—though

Snaggs, the Prime Minister, sound as a bell. Thinks a few informal conferences of the really enthusiastic might be held to discuss ways and means of rounding off this, the greatest of all national efforts. With this end in view he has arranged that I lunch to-morrow, alone, with the Bishop of Battersea at his Palace. That prim, dreary, side-whiskered bore! What a prospect!

September 5. Well! One never knows what surprises are in store for one! How wretched I thought that lunch with the Bishop would be: and how charming it was! We got on terms as soon as he had sent the menservants out of the room. I never connected the names, somehow, but that boy Cholmondeley at Oxbridge, my boy John's great friend, is the Bishop's son and the Bishop knew all about me. "So," said he, "we can talk as man to man"—and the token of our virility was the finest Madeira I have ever tasted in my life! But I must say I was rather shocked by his cynicism. I, in my innocence, have always thought that the time would come when all the prominent people who habitually break this law would come out in the open and demand its repeal. Not a bit of it: and the Bishop took it for granted that drink should be the regular privilege of the well-to-do and only the occasional indulgence of the poor. His parting words were: "Keep your eye on Irish Investments of all kinds. They've been going up steadily and they'll go up much more!"

September 6. The Bishop was right. Cheque for
£2,000 from Akenside with little personal note
enclosed saying, "Indigo Booming! R.A." Wonderful
how stimulating money is: did best leader of my life in
evening on splendid change in Ireland, prosperity due
to real agricultural co-operation, creameries, etc., with
moral to backward English farmers to combine, etc.
Letters, I admit, do pour in from public pointing out
whisky basis of Irish prosperity: but there's nothing like
not printing letters if you want to damp things down.

December 31. *New Year's Eve.* Did leading article
early. Felt sentimental and went off for lonely walk
around old haunts—"Five Bells," "Falstaff," "Three
Tuns," "Wheel and Pikestaff," "Compasses," "Marquis of Granby," etc. All now turned into shops or
cafés: only at the last, now some sort of warehouse, the
mouldering weather-worn sign still creaking in the
wind and rain, the indistinct effigy of a red-coated
eighteenth-century gentleman. How much of England
has passed with all that!—the gusto, the good cheer,
the drinking that really was drinking, i.e., nine-tenths
conversation. Getting sick of my morbid nostalgia
went to "Blue Moon," "Aladdin's Cave," and
"Jonah's Whale," all of which let me in although I was
not a member. Drinks in these rowdy holes not

trustworthy, except Irish whisky which is fairly reliable everywhere now, competition between distillers over there being still keen. Talking of Ireland, Briggs (who is in the Census Office) tells me next statistics as to population may be sensational, population of England actually diminishing as result of steady emigration of retired colonels, stock-brokers, unemployed, etc., to Ireland.

1924.—*January* 1. Well I'm hanged! He hasn't taken long about it. The Birthday Honours are out and Akenside has been made a peer, on account of "public and political services." "Lord Hurtley": trust him to do the thing properly and not fall back on that half-hearted subterfuge of making one's own surname baronial.

January 8. E. and I dined with Hurtleys at the Park. When the women had retired, Akenside told me he had retired also, so to speak. Wanted my advice. Had done all he needed to do for himself, helped to set Ireland on her feet, helped England over a very trying transitional time, now anxious to serve country before too old to be enterprising. Thought, and always had thought, Prohibition both farcical and dishonest. Had had private talk with Snaggs who quite agreed but thought Teetotal vote large enough to swing any election, so that no party could afford to offend it.

Snaggs added England traditional land of compromise, and pointed out that if J. Jones had been unable to make headway with his Pure Repeal views, Lady Astor had not been much more successful with her plea that if a law was on the statute-book it ought to be properly administered. Snaggs had finished up with, "Well, my boy, I'm too old now for such bold courses; but go ahead, and God bless you, though how you're going to do it *I* don't know." Akenside mooted an idea; I promised to think it over.

January 10. Snaggs excelled himself to-day at Leeds in his peroration denouncing those who "defy the statutory law of this ancient realm and are still—though largely in vain—attempting to poison our youth with the vile incubus which we shook off our backs six years ago—and for ever!" The old man keeps it up very well, considering the pace he's always gone.

June 13. After long delay Akenside launched campaign to-day in *Messenger*, which he has bought up. Points out, in leaders, news, cartoon and society columns, contrast between living conditions in Ireland to-day and those in England. Here, high taxes, much unemployment: in Ireland, no income-tax at all, no unemployment, sunny skies, and all the rest of it. The Shamrock is greener than ever; the Rose needs reviving by close contact with a younger civilisation.

New Party started—also subscription.

June 14. Sent small subscription to New Party, as in duty bound considering my last huge dividend from Indigo. Wrote leader attacking New Party as Party of Chimerical Project, which might even have certain Sinister Ulterior Aims.

June 15. Sir Elisha came in, raging. I plucked up spirit and shouted at him: "It seems impossible to please you, Sir Elisha." He then simmered down and explained that he really heartily sympathised with the New Party, the Party of Youth. Of course I couldn't understand, but I must go slow and be tactful.

June 16. Well I'm blowed! Dined at the Park, told Akenside my trouble, and learnt at last what the truth was, and how warily a man must walk in politics. Hurtley (Akenside) has sold out sixty per cent of his interest in Indigo to Sir Elisha, who has been after it for the last two years! If only Prohibition can be abolished in England, Irish whisky starts with a virtual monopoly. Campaign, mentioning only Prosperity, flourishing: candidates taking up cause everywhere.

September 29. Campaign going splendidly.

October 2. General Election announced.

November 13. We have won all the way along the line, my son John and young Cholmondeley having already been elected on a basis of Prosperity and the Anglo-Irish Entente.

November 21. Akenside Prime Minister! Who would have thought it! And in the Lords, too, after all I've always said about the impossibility of that.

1925.—*March* 18. Settled at last! England to be a Dominion of the Irish Empire, Free Trade between the two countries; D.O.R.A. to be abrogated. Sir Elisha to be Viceroy of England. Country in such a blaze of illuminations as has not been seen since Waterloo.

March 19. Lady Astor, in speech at Plymouth, said she would never be satisfied until Demon of Drink was chained. General exodus of night-club proprietors to America. Wrote leader pointing out Sir Elisha's promotion to highest office open to English citizen due reward of long and honourable services.

March 20. Rueful letter from John. Now settled down to serious work for Moral Sciences Examination. "Turned teetotaler: never really liked the beastly stuff."

BLAME ADAM AND EVE

BLAME ADAM AND EVE

I

THEY sat on either side of the drawing-room fire glooming at it, Charles Cartwright in a dinner-jacket, Dorothy softly gleaming in a pale blue sheath covered with dull spangles. Charles sat bored and staring, with his knotted hands clasped between his knees, the hollow eyes in his strong dark furrowed face, staring straight at the flames; looking every inch of what he was, both an admirable novelist and a man. He was intent, desperate, bewildered but still determined. He did not see the Dorothy who sat there, for he was looking at the Dorothy of his dreams, who had often, though not so often recently, come to life: the Dorothy who had instantaneously impressed herself upon him the very first time he had met her, at a luncheon-party, where nobody else seemed to be alive, much less to be living in the light of ideals. A luncheon-table, long ago. A dinner-table to-night. The last words that she had spoken at the dinner-table rang and rang through his head: "I simply can't understand how you can be so understanding as a novelist and so lacking in understanding as a man." "Rather hard-driving of one

243

word," reflected the critic in him, with a twist of the mouth. And then the yearning, tortured mate resumed: "Oh, damn the wretched girl—no, no, I won't even in thought use such a derogatory phrase about the noblest and dearest—why *can't* she see that a man *must* have rules and principles to live up to though he may be ever so compassionate to those who don't recognise them, or break them? Why *can't* she see that one may have all the heart in the world, and still realise that it is one's duty to face the facts of the world, half of which are unpleasant, including most of the facts about men and women? Oh, dear," he thought, with a sigh that he kept inaudible, "if only these goats of women would realise what we men are, and what the world is, and what the diversity of the world is, and how intractable are facts, and how we Englishmen have developed our hard faces simply through confronting them, but that we have confronted them from the most chivalrous motives in the world. What the hell," and his face twisted, and she watched it twisting, and she thought it was twisting out of dissatisfaction with her, her cooking, her management, her economy, her little efforts to have opinions of her own, which, after all, didn't matter, "what the hell did *she* know about India and the East?"

He checked himself. For that matter, he had never been to India and the East himself, though Ostend,

Switzerland and Seville he knew—at least the hotels, the casinos and the sights. But then he checked himself again.

Dorothy also looked into the fire. She did not look so intently as he, but more dreamily. She did not lean forward and stare fanatically, she reclined in her long armchair, with an elbow propped on the wooden rest, and her chin propped comfortably on her elbow—a chin as clean cut as the cheeks and brows, which framed the honest grey eyes and were framed themselves by the neat, straight, centrally-parted fair hair. "Why should he," she thought, "go on and on making a song about it? Why shouldn't she think, if she wanted to, that the Bolsheviks might be heralding a better world, that the Germans might be heralding a better world, that women should be allowed to do whatever they wanted to (and, after all, they only wanted to be faithful to a man who wedded them, however their thoughts might wander), and that Mr. Gandhi was a saint?" It was on that point, after dinner, that the conflict had come. She had said that Mr. Gandhi was a saint.

And Charles had broken out. Charles had said: "Yes, I daresay he is a saint; but he is a crook as well."

And she had replied: "How *can* you say that he is both a saint and a crook?" And he had replied; but she didn't understand his reply; and he, Charles, reflected on it still, as he gazed into the fire.

R

Charles Cartwright, still not speaking, gazed into the fire. He could, with his own sex, discuss any subject in the world until late at night: and late at night, under the influence of liquor, both parties would agree that they both meant the same thing and that, at any rate, they were both good fellows. With women, even with the noblest women in the world, it was different. Whatever you said, they always thought you were having a slap at them. "Omne ignotum pro magnifico": a Latin proverb: "everything unknown, people suppose to be wonderful." True enough, but immeasurably truer of women than of men. For himself he preferred old Dizzy's remark: "If you have imagination you do not need experience." The old Jew had made it, being a poet, when young; and had confirmed it, only more so, when old. He hadn't been to the East: but, good God, couldn't one *see* the East? Couldn't one understand that one side of Gandhi was a saint and one side a sophist? Couldn't one *see*, wasn't it *obvious*, that one side was a Tolstoyan and one side a twister? Couldn't one *see*, that for all his charm (not entirely physical) that the ascetic prophet was a fact-dodger, who thought on, "I'm sure they'll all love one another" lines, who would not face the untouchables, who would not face the appalling social conditions of Hindu India, who would not face the fact that there were seventy million Moslems who were at loggerheads with the Hindus and, physically, could wip them out in three months, who would not *see* that things must be gradual, that we began by policing India, that we continued by giving it sanitation, that, in spite of the polo and the pig-sticking, we were involved in a process which might gradually give it Christian and European ideas of honesty, humanity and decent living?

Again Charles heard, though she never spoke, her voice coming in: "You and your silly Christianity! I bet you would have treated Christ just as you want to treat Gandhi!"

He had answered: "The cases are not at all parallel. Quite apart from the fact that Christ was God, which I admit though you do not, I never saw a worse analogy. Pontius Pilate, and the washing of hands, and Pontius's wife! The Romans didn't mind Christ: in the end they made him. Do you really suppose that Lord Irwin would have executed Gandhi because the Brahmins had declared him blasphemous? My dear, you rather under-rate the British Empire!"

All that went on in Charles Cartwright's head as, with the muscles of his face growing tenser and tenser, he stared into the drawing-room fire.

But in Dorothy's head, all that went on was this: "Why on earth should Charles grow so angry, just because I said that Mr. Gandhi was a saint and a very nice man? Hang it all, just because one is a man's wife (and of course I admire him and think he's nearly always right) I don't see why one should always agree with everything he says. Besides, I *do* think that a great deal of what Mr. Gandhi says is *quite* right. I simply loathe those dull Anglo-Indian men with their rigid faces, and those hard Anglo-Indian women who (I don't mind betting) do a great deal more behind their husbands' backs than their husbands ever know— there *is* a certain excitement about fair-haired subalterns, although that silly darling old Charles could never, I'm sure, be brought to see it. Mr. Gandhi only says that India should be free. Why shouldn't India be free? Why shouldn't everybody be free? I simply *hate* all these restrictions which have come down to us from the past. I don't want to do anything outrageous, but I simply *don't* see why I shouldn't, if I don't do anybody else any harm."

And Charles thought: "If only she knew our sex." And Charles thought: "Oh, my darling, I must make one more attempt to get into contact with you. I simply can't *bear* that a love like ours—and we have such an awful lot in common—should break up simply because we differ about Gandhi or the Bolsheviks and all those ridiculous things beyond our horizon." And Charles said, impulsively and from the depths of his heart, "Darling."

And Dorothy replied: "Darling," with a certain frigid reservation that still did not quite close the road.

And Charles said: "Darling, it is simply loathsome that we should crash over a mere question of politics. But don't you see . . . ?"

And Dorothy said: "Oh, I'm simply sick of your saying 'Don't you see.' Don't *you* see that, although you may be right and you may be wrong, I want to think what *I* think, and not what *you* think."

And Charles said, looking up from the fire with such pathetic and appealing eyes, his face more finely cadaverous than ever in the firelight, "But, darling, it isn't a matter of what you think or what I think; can't you see that it is simply a matter of what *is*. For instance, what you said the other day about marriage."

"Well," said Dorothy, sheathed in the dress, and looking like virgin Diana in the glimmer of the fire, "what, I should like to know, *did* I say about marriage?"

"It was only this, darling," said Charles, with deliberate mildness, "that you said you didn't see why people shouldn't change their husbands and wives as they do their friends, if they want to."

Dorothy lowered her eyes, and her face looked sulky in the firelight. "And that's what I *do* think," said she, "if they want to. I only said if they want to."

Charles became even more amicable, deferential even, than before. "But, don't you see, darling . . ." he began.

"Oh, God," she spat, turning into a scaled snake, "I've had enough of your 'darling.' Why the hell can't you say what you mean instead of beating about the bush?"

He, at last exasperated into strength, at last responded. "Look here, Dorothy," he observed, "I don't very often play the still strong man, but you've damned well got to listen now." He rose and walked about the room while she lay motionless in her long chair. "If you want to say anything, say it," said she, "I'm used to listening."

"Well," said Charles firmly, "it's just this. I've always loved you, and I love you still."

"Can't that be taken as read?" replied Dorothy quietly. "I quite believe it, but it doesn't seem to make any difference. Of course, I know what it is really: you've been annoyed ever since I said I wanted to go out to dinner with the Fritzenheimers whom you can't stand, simply because they are Jews."

Charles raged on at her. "It's simply disgusting that you should say that," he protested; "you know damn well that half my friends are Jews. I know I've said that a lot of the Jews have more feeling for Jewry than for any of the artificial nations, as they think them, of Europe, but you jolly well know that I've never been prejudiced against any decent man because . . ."

"Yes," replied Dorothy, helping herself to a cigarette, "shouting as usual. Isn't it possible for you to discuss anything without shouting?"

Charles also sank, with a prodigious effort, into a

chair, and himself produced from a case, and laboriously lit, a cigarette. "Sorry, Dorothy, if I shouted,"
he said, "I was simply carried away. But it's a bit
rough, isn't it, when a man is trying to talk about
things in an impersonal way, to find a woman taking
things personally. I happen to hold certain views
about this life and the next, realism and the notions of
the ideologues as Napoleon called them: I also happen
to think that monogamy and chastity are good things,
and that most of us men are romantic enough, if only
you bloody modern women . . ."

She sprang from her chair, "Now I know—but of
course I've always known—what you really think in
your heart!" She shot at him forked lightnings of
anger and flounced through the door.

Charles Cartwright looked into the fire in a sad,
puzzled way. He drank a whisky or two, and then he
also went up to his bedroom. They had separate
bedrooms: they had both, from the start, believed that
married people ought not to interfere with each other.
To such an extent had they believed this that they had
not even had any children.

II

Dorothy, once more, and for the last time, despair-
ingly, went up to her bedroom: but not to bed. She

hesitated for a long time. She had really loved
Charles when she first met him, and, in spite of all his
maddening faults, she loved him still. But *how* could
he be so lacking in understanding of women; *how*
could he be so unable to compromise? She herself had
no very positive knowledge about the Bolsheviks and
Mr. Gandhi: as for the history of marriage, she was
quite willing to believe that Charles was quite right
when he said that women were damned lucky (why
would he always say "damned"?) to have imposed
monogamy upon men, that marriage was invented for
women's sakes, and that if she ever persuaded him that
"affairs" didn't much matter he would go off and have
a hundred of them himself. But, why would he insist
on calling an affair "adultery"? Look at poor Mrs.
Hawkins next door: young and pretty, with a disgusting, fat, drunken husband; why would it be wrong for
her to have a lover when all she wanted was love,
which she didn't get? When she first met Charles he
seemed so different; and now he was so hard and set.
She had been captivated by Charles at first sight; but
wouldn't it have been better if, after all, she had taken
the plunge and met that man, whom she had never
met, and who had begged and begged her to meet him?

*   *   *   *

"Box XY2" it had been, in *The Times* Agony
Column. Somebody had advertised out of the blue

saying that he was lonely, that he only wanted cor-
respondence, and that, as proof of his *bona fides*, he
would guarantee never to seek a meeting with his
correspondent. She had been at home then, a very
young matron to her father's prep. school; and, with
her heart fluttering, she had answered. A letter had
come back, so deferential, decent and inquiring; with
the assurance repeated that no meeting was sought.
She had replied, giving (as a young woman can, when
she knows her grounds) a certain measure of consolation. He had replied again thanking her from the
bottom of his heart, and talking about books and the
world. She, wanting to know about books and the
world, had paraded her poor knowledge, and asked,
catechismically, for more information. So they had
gone on. He never revealed his identity. He never
would. He wrote so understandingly—more understandingly than any man whom she had ever met. He
talked of flowers and museums; he held before her
eyes visions of their visiting museums and gardens
together; he, shrinking from women, apparently,
talked of what might be if only the world were
different from what it was. He wrote, "Oh, if . . ."
and there was the implication, "I dare not, lest both of
us be disappointed, though both of us, ephemeral
creatures, under the vast mysterious sky, hanker only
after love and comfort and a mutual sinking into one
another . . . and delight, also, but that as something

thrown in, to which one has no claim." And then his letters had stopped. They had stopped at just the right moment. For they had stopped just when she had met Charles Cartwright. So quick, so sympathetic with women, so humorous, so interested in the beautiful, so fond of flowers, so anxious to please and to show her all the museums. If only Charles had been all that he seemed to be—or if only she had taken the extreme step and met her correspondent!

She moved from her chair and went to her desk, her whole soul crying in her: "Can't I have a second chance? Why can't women have a second chance?" It was extravagantly unlikely that he, the unknown, the perfectly sympathetic, the utterly considerate, would still be watching the columns of *The Times*. Even if he was he might have scruples about another man's wife: these men having such a dreadful sense of property. But he might, he might, and this had now got beyond bearing! Why, even this evening, Charles had recommended her to consider the first few chapters of Genesis. He had said: "It would be all right in Eden, where there was no marriage and the fruits dropped off the bough, and the lion grazed beside the lamb. But that myth means nothing. An even greater poet than Shakespeare wrote it. 'You shall earn your bread by the sweat of the brow,'" Charles had said; and deduced from it, in his maddening, masculine way, the whole structure of civilisation, social and sexual.

Dorothy almost screamed. She *didn't* want to be unfaithful. Besides, she *did* love Charles. But it was *awful* to listen to his theories; and it was *awful* to feel that woman must always be dependent upon man. Working herself up and up, getting more and more into a frenzy, she got to the point at which she said to herself: "I simply *won't* be tyrannised over any more. There was that nice man I corresponded with all those years ago. I've never met another man who would quite understand, but I'm sure that one would. Why *shouldn't* I write to him? Why *should* this silly institution of marriage preclude me? Why *should* I be bound by all these wretched vows that men have invented for a world of men?"

III

So she wrote. It was just at the time that he was looking for it. "Elaine" appeared in the Agony Column after all those years; and "Lanalot" after all those years responded. Neither had looked at that column for years; but each resumed the examination of it at the same time. There was a tentative answer and a tentative reply. Ultimately, both parties feeling guilty, and both parties (in point of fact) half re-solved to get a slight "kick" out of the meeting, and no more, there was an assignation.

Charles arrived at Sloane Square Station first. He was five minutes early. He almost left. "Why," thought he, "should I be meeting this complete stranger here, probably a governess with eczema, when I've got my darling Dorothy at home, who is worth all the women in the world?" Then honour crept in. "Well," thought he, "I can't let a woman down. I promised to meet her here, both wearing red carnations, and here I'll have to be, and stick it out." He became more and more nervous; and then, on the stroke of the hour, he saw walking out of the gangway, wearing another red carnation . . . good God, Dorothy!

Had he not been petrified, he would have run. He could not run. No such impulse came to Dorothy. She walked up to him, as cool as a cucumber, and said: "Hello, Charles, what are you doing here?" His mouth dry, as after a night's debauch, and his lips hardly able to separate, he whispered: "Nothing; I was just meeting a friend. Wha-a-at are you doing here?"

Dorothy replied brightly: "Oh, I thought Ena Waring would be here. She promised to meet me."

They waited for ten minutes. Then they went to tea at Rumpelmayer's. She knew, but she never spoke a word. So, after a longer delay, did he know. Nor did he speak a word. But awake that night, he murmured to himself: "Blame Adam and Eve."